Gone

(Book Six in the *Chop, Chop* Series)

by

L.N. Cronk

Front Cover Photography by photoGartner.
Back Cover Photography by Y-Image.

Spanish translations provided by Vicki Oliver Krueger.

Scripture taken from the HOLY BIBLE, NEW
INTERNATIONAL VERSION ®. Copyright © 1973, 1978, 1984
by International Bible Society. Used by permission of Zondervan. All
rights reserved.

ISBN Number: 978-0-9820027-8-0

Published by Rivulet Publishing
West Jefferson, NC, 28694, U.S.A.

For Jim, Val and June,
Pat, Regena, and Tina.

Now there is in store for me the crown of righteousness, which the Lord, the righteous Judge, will award to me on that day – and not only to me, but also to all who have longed for his appearing. 2 Timothy 4:8

Author's Note:

IMPORTANT! I want you to know going into this story that it is likely to leave you with more questions, than answers. This novel, *Gone*, is David's last story, and it takes place approximately twenty years after David decided to move his family back to Mexico at the end of *The Other Mothers*. A lot of things have happened during that time, but those things won't be discussed by David . . . only hinted at.

All of those questions will be answered, however, by Jordan and Tanner (in *Not Quickly Broken* and *Alone*, respectively). I hope you will enjoy this novel for what it is – David's final attempt to be the man God wants him to be – and that you will then read Jordan and Tanner's stories, to fill in all the blanks.

I also hope that you will take a few moments to leave reviews for the books, if you haven't done so already. Reviews are immensely important for continuing to let others know about the series and I appreciate each and every one of them. Reviews for the first book in the series, *Chop, Chop*, are the most important, but reviews for the sequels are valuable as well and if you have time to review all of them, it would be much appreciated!

I thank you sincerely for reading the novels in the *Chop, Chop* series so far and hope you continue to enjoy them. I pray that they will be a blessing to you, as each of you are to me.

In Christ's love,
L.N. Cronk

~ ~ ~

SOMEONE WAS LAYING on their horn and — for some reason — I was shaking. Looking ahead, I saw a driveway and pulled in.

I turned the car off, rubbed my forehead, and sat there until I'd calmed down a bit. Then I sighed and looked around.

Where *was* I?

A woman came out of the house and walked toward the car, staring at me suspiciously.

I rolled down my window.

"*Hola*," I said, trying to look as friendly as possible.

She nodded.

"*Me puedes decir como llegar a . . .*"

Can you tell me how to get to . . .

I wasn't really sure what to ask her because I was so lost. I finally decided I'd better just get to Zocaló in the heart of Mexico City because I could get *anywhere* from there.

"*¿Plaza de la Constitución el Zocaló?*" I finally asked.

She looked at me strangely and finally pointed.

"*Ve por ese camino . . . vira a la derecha a la Carretera Federal Ochenta y Cinco. Mantenga en esa dirección algunos treinta minutos y debería ver unos señales de tránsito.*"

Go that way . . . turn right onto Highway 85. Stay on that for about thirty minutes and you should see some signs.

Thirty minutes?

I *lived* thirty minutes from Zocaló. And I was going to have another thirty minutes to go on top of that?

I thanked her, pulled away, and sighed again, hoping I'd recognize something along the way.

I didn't.

3

Half an hour later I finally saw the Metropolitan Cathedral and was surprised at the rush of relief I felt. I turned right onto Medero and drove for a while.

Beginning to relax, I realized how hungry I was. I pulled in to the same McDonald's where I'd bought a thousand Happy Meals. I ordered a double cheeseburger, large fries, and a drink and started home.

When I finally arrived I was surprised to find the door open. Laci was usually pretty good about locking up before she left.

Oh well.

I crammed my McDonald's bag into the trash, headed down the hall to my office, and got to work.

By dinnertime Laci wasn't home, so I called her.

"I'm working late tonight, remember?"

"You are?"

"Yes . . . we talked about it this morning."

"Oh," I said. "I guess I forgot. What am I supposed to do for dinner?"

"I told you I left some meatloaf and potatoes on a plate in the fridge for you to heat up."

I opened the fridge and looked around.

"There's nothing here," I told her.

There was a long pause.

"Are you sure?"

"Of course I'm sure."

"Did you eat it for lunch?"

"No," I said. "I went to McDonald's for lunch."

There was another long pause.

"I'm gonna come home," she said.

"No, Laci," I said. "It's no big deal. I'll find something to eat."

"No," she said. "I'll pick up something and bring it home."

"That's ridiculous, Laci," I said. "I don't need you to come home. You stay there and get done whatever you need to get done. I'll find myself something to eat."

"Are you sure?"

"Sure, I'm sure," I said. "I'm perfectly capable of taking care of myself."

The next night the table was set for three.

"We're having company?" I asked.

"Dorito's coming for dinner."

Dorito's real name was Doroteo. He was the only one of our children who still lived near us.

"Just Dorito?" I asked, disappointed that his wife and girls weren't coming.

"Ayla has a soccer game," she explained.

"And Dorito's not going to it?" I asked.

"He's coming for dinner," she said again.

Obviously.

He came in the door just as Laci was dishing up dinner and hugged me.

"Hi, Dad," he said as I pounded him on the back.

"How you doing?" I asked.

"Fine," he said, turning to Laci. He gave her what seemed like an extra-long hug.

During dinner I tried to ask him about the kids and about work, but he was very quiet (not a word usually used to describe Dorito).

"So, how come you aren't at Ayla's game?" I asked.

"I just . . . I just wanted to see you guys," he shrugged, looking down at his plate.

"Dorito," I finally asked. "Is everything okay?"

"Sure, Dad," he nodded, not looking up from his plate.

I put down my fork.

"Obviously not," I said. "What's wrong?"

I saw him take a breath and then look up at Laci for help. That's when I realized she was already in on this.

"Would somebody care to tell me what's going on?" I asked.

Dorito pushed his chair away from the table. He went to the freezer and got some ice for his glass.

I looked at Laci expectantly.

"We just wanted to talk to you about something," she finally said. "But I thought we'd wait until after dinner."

"Well, you might as well just talk to me about it now," I said.

Laci looked up at Dorito. Dorito looked back at her and then set his glass down.

"Are the girls okay?" I asked, unable to keep panic from sneaking into my voice. "Is somebody sick?"

"No, no," Dorito assured me, sitting back down and putting a hand on my shoulder. "Everybody's fine."

"So what's this all about then?"

"David," Laci said gently, looking at me and putting her hand on mine. "We're just . . . we've just been a bit worried about you, that's all."

"About me?"

I laughed as my panic quickly subsided. "Why would you be worried about me?"

"You seem a little . . . distracted lately," she said carefully.

"What do you mean?"

"I mean . . . like you're not paying attention to things the way you used to."

"I guess my mind's just been on the addition," I told her.

The orphanage where Laci worked (and where half of our children had come from) had just received the funding they needed to add a huge new wing. The firm I worked for was in charge of the project and I was going to be the lead engineer – Dorito was going to be the lead architect.

"I've just been thinking about it a lot lately," I assured her. "I'm excited about it!"

"No," Laci said, shaking her head. "This has been going on longer than that."

"What are you talking about?"

"I mean . . . I mean, you're doing things that aren't . . . right."

"Things that aren't *right?*"

"Not . . . normal," she said hesitantly.

"Normal . . ."

She nodded.

"Such as?"

She quickly glanced at Dorito before she went on.

"I tell you things, David, and then later you don't even remember that we talked."

"Everybody does that sometimes."

"Yes," she agreed, "*sometimes* . . . but you're doing it a lot more than just sometimes."

"You're making a big deal out of nothing," I said, waving my hand at her dismissively.

"That's not all," Laci said.

"What?"

"Do you remember a couple of weeks ago when I came home and you were out in the driveway in the car?"

"Yes," I lied.

"Well, you were just *sitting* there!" she said. "And I think you'd *been* sitting there for a long time."

"No I hadn't," I told her. "I was just thinking about something! I've had a lot on my mind."

She sighed and I looked at Dorito.

"I've been fine, haven't I?" I asked him.

"You haven't . . . you haven't been yourself lately," he answered.

"Oh, brother," I said, rolling my eyes. "This is ridiculous. I can't believe she's got you convinced that something's wrong too."

"We want you to go see a doctor," Laci said. "Just go have a check-up, make sure everything's okay."

"So you think I'm crazy?"

"No!" Laci insisted. "I don't think you're crazy at all! I think – I just think maybe something's stressing you out or something and that we should talk to a doctor about it."

"Right now," I said, "*you're* stressing me out."

"Look," Dorito said. "Why don't you just go see a doctor and make Mom feel better?"

"Fine," I agreed. "But I'm not going to some quack doctor who got his medical degree off the back of a cereal box. When we go home next summer I'll tell Dr. Taylor that you're worried."

The doctors we had available to us in Mexico City really weren't that bad, but I didn't go to one of them unless I really had to. We went back to the States often enough that I could schedule any annual check-up type stuff when we were home.

"Mike doesn't think this needs to wait six months," Laci said.

"You called *Mike* about this?" I yelled. Mike was one of my best friends. He also happened to be a physician.

"I just wanted to—"

"You had *NO* right to do that Laci!" I shouted, slamming my hand down on the table. Laci jumped. "There's nothing wrong with me!"

"Dad—"

"You stay out of this!" I yelled.

"Dad," Dorito persisted, "I came over here last month to trim for you and you'd filled the weed eater up with milk."

"I did not!"

"*Yes*, you did. There was a jug of rancid milk sitting right next to it."

"Who asked you for your help anyway?" I snapped at him. "I can take care of my own yard – you leave my weed eater alone!"

"Your weed eater is *ruined*," Dorito muttered under his breath.

"Well, I didn't do it!" I cried. "*Somebody* might have done it, but it wasn't me!"

"Who would have touched your weed eater?" Laci asked.

"Maybe you did it," I accused her.

"Why would I do that?"

I decided I'd better back off before they accused me of being paranoid, too.

"I don't know, Laci. What I'm saying is, why would *I* have done it?"

"Grace told me she called you Monday," Dorito went on. "She said . . . she said you acted like you didn't even know who she was!"

"You think I don't know my own kids?" I cried. I started ticking them off on my fingers. "There's *Grace* and *Marco* and *Meredith* and *Lily* and *Amber*–"

"David," Laci interrupted worriedly, "Monday you went to the store to get some bread and you were gone for *five* hours! You wouldn't answer your phone and when you finally came home you didn't have any bread."

I had absolutely no idea what she was talking about.

"So, because my phone wasn't working right and I forgot some bread you're ready to lock me up?"

"No one said anything about locking you up! All we want is for you to go to the doctor to see if they can figure out what's going on."

"Nothing's going on! I'm fine and I don't need a doctor to tell me that I'm fine!"

"What's it gonna hurt to go see a doctor?" Dorito asked. "If you're so sure you're fine, then why don't you just humor us and go to the doctor?"

"No," I said, standing up. "If you're still worried about it next summer then I'll talk to Dr. Taylor, but I don't want to hear another word about it until then. Do you understand?"

"But–" Laci started.

"Not another word!"

"Please sit down, David," she pleaded. "I won't talk about it anymore. Sit down and finish your dinner."

"I've lost my appetite," I told her and I stalked away.

At two in the morning I got out of bed.

"Where're you going?" Laci asked.

"I'm going to go get that *bread* that you wanted," I muttered under my breath.

"What?"

"I'm getting some cough medicine, Laci."

"You haven't been coughing."

"Yes, I have. I don't feel good."

I rifled around in the medicine cabinet until I found a bottle that was left over from when one of us had had bronchitis or something.

Do not take except under the supervision of a physician. Do not operate a motor vehicle or heavy machinery when taking this medicine.

Warning:

This medication causes drowsiness.

That sounded good.

I measured out the recommended dosage, tossed my head back, and gulped it down.

The next day I was in my office going over the survey of the property for the new wing. I opened my bottom desk drawer to get a file and found a bunch of forks, knives, and spoons. I stared at them for a minute and then I took them to the kitchen and put them away, making sure each piece went exactly where it had come from.

That night I lay in bed until just after midnight. I got up and went to the medicine cabinet, poured myself a double shot of cough medicine, and crawled back into bed.

For the next week nothing else happened.
Laci didn't say another word about it.
I stayed away from the cough medicine.

Nine days after Laci and Dorito's "intervention," I was in the bedroom.

I heard a noise coming from the kitchen and I walked down the hall to investigate.

Water was pouring full blast from the faucet and both sinks were overflowing. The water flowed in a slow waterfall over the counter and onto the floor.

I shut the water off and sopped it all up with towels.

Then I went to the Laundromat.

That night I finished off the cough syrup.

Two days later, my phone rang. It was my supervisor, Josef.

"Hi, Josef."

"Hi, David," he said.

"What's up?"

"Well," he said, hesitating, "I wanted to talk to you about Hartman Station."

"Yeah? I sent the stuff up there a few days ago . . . you should have gotten it by now."

"We got it, Dave," he hesitated again. "But there's a problem — the ratios for most of the casings are way off."

"They are?" I asked, wandering over to my desk. I found the Hartman project and tried to find the specification pages.

"And the girder spacing on the portico isn't calculated right."

I found the spec section and started looking at the numbers.

"I'll fix this and send it right away," I told him, although I couldn't remember how to calculate them or imagine how I was possibly going to fix them.

"Dave," Josef was saying, "we'd like to fly you up to Chicago."

"Why?"

"We'd just like to meet with you and talk about what's going on."

"Whatdya mean, *'What's going on'*? Is this a big deal? I just made a few mistakes. I'll fix it and send you what you need this afternoon."

There was no way I could ever have it ready by this afternoon.

"Dave . . ."

"What?"

12

"Stuff like this has been happening a bit over the past few months. We really need to talk about it."

I sat on the couch, stared at the floor, and waited for Laci. When she walked in the door I looked up at her. She stopped in her tracks and looked back at me. We stared at each other for a long moment.

Finally I nodded at her.

"I'll go," I said.

~ ~ ~

OVER THE PAST twenty years (when I'd had a sore throat or tendonitis or something) I had, on occasion, seen a physician in Mexico City named Dr. Reyes and – once I agreed to go to a doctor – Laci scheduled an appointment with him. When Dr. Reyes couldn't find anything wrong with me (by hitting my knee with a hammer, shining a light in my eye, and gagging me with a popsicle stick) he referred me to a neurologist.

"His name is Lorenzo Soto," Dr. Reyes said. "I think you'll like him – he did his residency at Duke University."

"In North Carolina?"

"No," Dr. Reyes said wryly. "The Duke University that's in Tijuana."

Like the appointment with Dr. Reyes, Laci was with me when I saw Dr. Soto. After she explained to him in a nervous voice what had been going on, he asked me some questions.

"Have either of your parents suffered from dementia?"

"Well, maybe my father," I said. "He had a stroke about a year ago and he's in a nursing home now. It's really hard to communicate with him . . . he doesn't seem to know what's going on a lot of the time, but it's hard to tell."

"But he's never had an official diagnosis of Alzheimer's or anything like that?"

I shook my head. "He was fine before he had the stroke."

"What about your mother?"

"She died from a pulmonary embolism when she was fifty-seven," Laci told him.

The doctor nodded.

"So," he said, "it's possible that your mother had Alzheimer's, but died before she became symptomatic?"

"You think I have *Alzheimer's?*"

"No, not necessarily," he said. "These symptoms can be an indication of other problems as well, but Alzheimer's is definitely one of the things that we need to consider."

"But he's too young to have Alzheimer's," Laci protested.

"It's rare for someone in their early fifties to be diagnosed with Alzheimer's," he acknowledged, "but it can certainly happen. It's called early-onset Alzheimer's."

"Early-onset Alzheimer's?"

"That's what we call it when it's diagnosed in a patient under age sixty-five. It can even appear in patients under the age of forty, but that's extremely rare."

"You said that's just one of the things that could be causing this," I said. "What else might it be?"

"Well, it's possible that you're suffering from small strokes that are producing these symptoms. We also need to rule out cerebrovascular disease, blood clots, thyroid problems, a brain tumor . . ."

With the small exception of thyroid problems, none of this was sounding too promising.

"Stress," he went on, "depression, fatigue . . ."

Those sounded better.

"Or . . ." he said.

"Or what?"

"Or," he shrugged. "It could be nothing."

"Did you hear what he said?" Laci asked on the way home. "It could be nothing . . ."

"Yeah," I said. "Or it could be a whole lotta other things."

"But a lot of them are very treatable . . . like what if it's just stress? I'll bet it's just stress."

"It's not stress!" I told her. She looked at me. "Laci, I'm happier than I've ever been in my whole life. The kids are out on their own, doing great . . . I'm at the point now where I can pick the projects I want at work . . . I'm getting to work with Dorito on the new wing . . ." *I'm married to you* . . . "What exactly do you think I'm stressed about?" I went on, glancing at her.

"I don't know," she said quietly. "But maybe we just need a vacation."

That evening, I called Mike.

"They did a bunch of tests," I told him.

"Like what?"

"I don't know," I said. "They took about a gallon of blood and he said something about genetic testing and thyroid levels and liver function and then they did an MRI and a PET scan and I'm supposed to have spinal fluid drawn tomorrow, which – I gotta tell ya – doesn't sound like a whole lot of fun . . ."

"If you want to come home," Mike said, "you can give me your doctor's info and we can get all your test results sent up here. I can get you in with Dr. Keener at the Mayo Clinic. He's a great guy – I've known him since med school."

"You think I should come home?"

"He's one of the best neurologists in the world. I mean . . . it's up to you, but if it were me I'd want to see Dr. Keener."

I hesitated.

16

"You could stay with me and Danica," he offered. "We haven't gotten together with you guys for a long time and it'd be great to see you . . ."

"Yeah," I agreed. "I guess it wouldn't hurt for us to take a vacation."

We made arrangements for Dr. Soto to send all of my test results to the Mayo Clinic, bought our plane tickets, and packed our bags.

I had always considered the United States to be my home and – as always – I was anxious to leave Mexico.

If I had known, however, as I pulled out of the driveway, that I would never be returning to the house where we'd raised our six children and spent almost half of our lives, would I have felt differently? Would I have shed a tear if I'd known that one day Dorito and his wife were going to have to come in and clean it out for us? If I'd know that I would never set foot on Mexican soil again . . . would I have been sad?

Yes.

~ ~ ~

WE GOT TO Minnesota on Sunday evening and Mike and Danica met us at the airport. I could tell from the way that they were acting that whatever Laci had filled their heads with had them both really worried, but I tried not to let it get to me. There'd been one isolated incident at work and that was it (except for somehow winding up half of an hour on the other side of Zocaló, the silverware in my desk drawer, and the sink overflowing).

Nothing to worry about at all.

We had an appointment with Dr. Keener at seven-thirty the next morning. I had the distinct impression that he normally started his day at eight and that he was meeting with us early only because he was friends with Mike and was doing him a favor. He unlocked the door to his office for us himself (his receptionist was hanging her purse up in a closet when we walked by her window).

"You're going to have a lot of testing done today," he began.

"Not another spinal tap, I hope," I said.

"No. We have the results from the one you had done in Mexico and we can use those. We've also received the results from the blood work and DNA testing."

"What did they show?" Laci asked anxiously, leaning forward.

"Let's wait and discuss all of the results tomorrow after we have a complete picture to look at."

Laci nodded tightly and sat back.

"I've scheduled you to have a battery of neurocognitive tests today and a neuropsychological evaluation and I'd like to have another MRI done – this time with contrast."

That was fine with me. I could lie still for twenty minutes listening to that thing banging and clanking around me just fine . . . as long as I didn't have to have another *lumbar puncture*.

The MRI with contrast was going to be done at an imaging center about a quarter of a mile away, and then I would come back to Dr. Keener's clinic for the rest of the tests.

"With contrast" meant that after they did the preliminary MRI scan they pulled me back out of the tube and injected me with something. Then they slid me back into the tube and did a bunch of sequences of scans. In between each sequence the machine was humming, but while the sequences were actually being taken, it sounded like a road crew. I had earplugs, but they didn't help much.

After I was done with the MRI, I went out into the lobby where Laci was waiting for me. We got into our rental car and drove back to Dr. Keener's clinic.

I saw three different people while I was at the clinic. The first one was a woman who gave me all the cognitive tests.

"First," she said, "we are going to administer a very short test called the Blessed Test."

"The *Blessed* Test?" I asked and she smiled. "Why's it called that?"

"It's named after the man who developed it."

I nodded.

"Are you ready?" she asked, and I nodded again.

She started out by asking me all sorts of normal stuff like my age, address, phone number, what year, month, day, and hour it was. Then I had to say all the months of the year backward, count from one to twenty and later backward from twenty to one (all of which I happened to nail). She wanted to know who the president of the United States was (duh). Who was the prime minister? *Of which country?* I asked. *Of Great Britain,* she told me. I answered her and then threw in the prime minister of Israel for good measure.

After that we moved on to some other tests. I had to draw an analog clock with the face, numbers, and hands. I had to take a computerized test with a touchscreen that tested my memory and concentration. I had to draw pictures with different patterns on them. I also got to do some math.

After she was finished with me, I went down the hall and into another room that had some exercise equipment and mats and stuff in it. Some guy came in and tested me by having me complete a bunch of physical tasks. I felt like someone who had just been pulled over by a policeman under suspicion of drunk driving. *Lift your right arm straight out in front of you. Follow this light with only your eyes. Lace your fingers behind your back. Walk this line.*

After that he asked me to tie and untie my shoes . . . had me unbuckle and then buckle my belt . . . gave me a pair of gloves and asked me to put them on. I had to stack blocks by looking at a picture and copying the structure that I saw and bounce a ball back and forth with him like we were playing four-square.

Finally I went to *another* examining room and got turned over to a third person, who asked me all kinds of questions about how I was feeling. Was I more tired than normal? Was I sleeping well at night? Was I worried about anything? *(Uhhh, yeah, I'm worried that apparently my brain isn't working right.)* Did I think I was depressed? Did I ever hear voices? Had I ever thought about harming or killing myself? Harming or killing others? Had anything traumatic happened to me recently?

And during some of this time, Laci was in another room, answering all sorts of questions too.

When we were finally done it was after two o'clock and I was starving.

"Let's go get some lunch," I suggested, and Laci nodded. At the restaurant, however, she didn't order anything. After the waitress left, I asked her, "Did you already eat while I was being tested?"

"No," she said, shaking her head. "I'm just not hungry."

"Come on, Laci. Ya gotta eat!"

"I can't," she said in a small voice.

I got up and grabbed another menu and put it down in front of her.

"Order something," I said, tapping the menu. "You don't need to be worried – everything went really, really good today."

She looked at me doubtfully.

"It did!" I insisted. "All those tests I did at the clinic – counting backward and remembering patterns and stuff – I nailed it. And I haven't been doing anything weird lately, have I?"

"No," she admitted.

"When's the last time I did something that wasn't right?"

"I guess . . . I guess about a week ago," she said.

"So whatever it was was probably just a fluke – I'm fine!" I said, tapping the menu again. "Please pick something to eat."

She nodded reluctantly and looked down at her menu. She didn't remind me that I'd had other periods of time where I'd seemed *fine* too, but that the problems kept coming back. She didn't wonder aloud why the doctor had ordered another MRI if the first one had been *fine*. She didn't question why we hadn't been told the results of all the testing that had already come back if everything was so *fine*.

That evening, Danica and Mike went all out, making us a special dinner. We had cantaloupe wrapped in prosciutto, salad with jicama and goat cheese, sautéed asparagus, garlic stuffed potatoes, grilled filet mignon, and lobster tails with butter.

After we ate, I felt stuffed . . . *happy*. We settled back in chairs in the living room, watching the embers glowing in the fireplace.

Then – suddenly – Mike was squatted down next to me with his hand on my knee. Over his shoulder I could see Laci, crying softly, and Danica trying to console her.

"What's going on?" I asked him.

Mike narrowed his eyes at me.

"Do you know where you are?" he asked.

"Of course I know where I am!" (What a stupid question.) *"What's going on?"* I asked again.

"You were . . ." Mike hesitated. "You were confused for a few minutes, that's all."

I glanced at Laci, who was trying to wipe away evidence that she had been crying. Danica was still talking to her quietly.

"Confused how?" I asked.

"Well," Mike said gently. "You wanted some dessert."

"But we just had cake," I pointed out.

"I know," Mike agreed, "but you didn't remember that. You kept asking for a red freezer pop."

"Really?"

"See?" Laci asked in a shrill voice. "This is *exactly* what I've been talking about!"

Mike turned to her and gave her a look that I think he intended to silence her. He turned back to me.

"It's okay, David," he said reassuringly, patting me on the knee. "Do you know what day it is?"

"Yes!" I said irritably. "It's Monday. We spent all day at the doctor. We're getting the results back tomorrow, which happens to be *Tuesday*, unless they've changed things around and haven't told me about it."

He smiled at me.

"Do you know who I am?"

"You're Mike, the witch doctor."

He smiled again and removed his hand from my knee.

That was the first time I was actually aware that something had happened – the first time I knew that I had been . . . *gone*.

Unfortunately, it wouldn't be the last.

~ ~ ~

THE RESULTS THE next morning were not going to be good.

That evening, for the first time – lying there in bed – I realized this with certainty. Before now, I think I had been clinging to what Dr. Soto had told me: *It could be nothing.* Although I'd had people telling me that things weren't right, I had felt so normal that I'd convinced myself everything was okay. Plus, Laci had admitted that nothing had happened in about a week.

But what had occurred after dinner a few hours ago had *not* been right, and I now knew for certain what Laci had apparently known for weeks – something was wrong.

Really, *really* wrong.

This was a frightening realization and with it came a painful flutter in the pit of my stomach and a shortness of breath that no amount of cough medicine was ever going to fix.

Every morning when we got up and every evening before we went to bed, Laci and I would kneel down on the floor together and pray. It was something we had done ever since we had gotten married. And so, this evening – like always – we'd prayed together. But I'd been completely disconnected . . . like a wooden marionette, simply going through the motions.

I tried to pray again now, but it wasn't going to happen, so I lay there in the darkness feeling more alone than I ever had in my entire life.

Of course I wasn't alone – Laci was lying right there next to me – but I *felt* very alone. And panicked. And scared.

This cannot be happening. This cannot be happening.

24

But it was.

My mind drifted to a time when I was in college. There'd been a woman at the church I went to who'd had a brain tumor. I remembered praying for her with my Bible study group and I remembered that she would show up periodically for a Sunday service or a church picnic and then she'd disappear again for a few weeks and we'd get further prayer requests, detailing her apparently hopeless battle. They'd done surgery and chemotherapy and radiation and then more surgery and more chemotherapy and more radiation and then even more.

After each surgery she had looked worse and worse. First they had just shaved part of her head and put a bunch of metal stitches in. Then they'd done the chemo and radiation. She'd lost all of her hair and arrived at church looking feeble and drained, the skin where they'd done the radiation looking painfully bright red. During the next surgery they had removed part of her skull or something and she was left with a big dent in her head. The last surgery she endured had relegated her to a wheelchair, and – after that – they'd finally left her alone and let her die in peace.

She had lived for about nine months after her first surgery and had been so sick and so miserable for most of her time after that that I couldn't help but wonder – if she had *known* that all the treatments and surgeries weren't going to work . . . if she had *known* that she was going to die anyway – would she have still fought so valiantly? Would it have been better for her to spend her last few months enjoying what time she had left with her loved ones instead of sitting in hospital rooms, waiting for and enduring treatments that were only going to make her feel worse?

If there wasn't a good chance, a really, really good chance, that I would get better, I had thought at the time, *I would not want to go through all that.*

But now – faced with such a possibility – was I really ready to give up so easily and die? I lay there and thought about how much I was willing to bear and how much I would be willing to fight.

After thinking about it for a while, it became clear to me that – if I was going to die anyway – I did not want to spend the rest of my life sick and miserable the way she had.

Of course that meant *dying*. This also is not a whole lot of fun to think about (particularly when you find yourself feeling all alone and completely unable to pray).

After a long while though, I finally decided that if I had a brain tumor or something and there was a greater than fifty percent chance that I could beat it, I'd take the treatments and do whatever it took to fight. Otherwise, I was just going to enjoy what little time I had left. That, I decided, was my cutoff point – fifty percent.

My thoughts turned to Laci. I could tell by the sound of her breathing that she wasn't asleep either. I closed my eyes and wondered how Laci would feel about my fifty percent decision.

Not good. I knew that she would want me to fight no matter how small my chances were.

But it was my life, and if I didn't want to spend the rest of it undergoing treatments that were going to make me feel terrible and not help anyway, well, she was going to have to accept that. I'd just have to put my foot down.

Suddenly Laci sat up in bed.

"What's the matter?" I asked

"Nothing," she said, swinging her legs over the side of the bed. "I have to go to the bathroom."

The bathroom was down the hall, and since we weren't very familiar with Mike and Danica's house, I sat up too and turned the light on for her. Laci got out of bed and went into the hall.

After she was gone I looked around the room. Something about having the light on made it easier to breathe – made me feel less panicky. I remembered how Amber had often wanted the light left on when she was scared at night. Somehow it had made her feel safer and now I knew exactly how she'd felt. I left the light on and lay back down.

After a few minutes, Laci returned and climbed back into bed. She lay down beside me on her back and I moved closer to her, putting my head on her shoulder and my arm over her. She wrapped an arm around me, too.

It was when she didn't say anything – didn't ask me to turn out the light (and didn't even ask me why I was leaving it on) – that I realized she was just as scared as I was and that having the light on was making her feel better too.

Poor Laci. Had she had this horrible feeling of dread in the pit of her stomach for a month?

Dear God, I prayed, *please be with Laci. Please help her through this . . . please give her peace and help her to not be scared.*

Earlier when I'd tried to pray I had gotten nowhere, but now – now that I was praying for *Laci* instead of myself (or maybe it was because the light was on) – I could do it.

Wow.

The fear and dread that had been overwhelming only a few minutes earlier lifted. I gave Laci a little hug and she squeezed me back.

And I kept on praying.

At some point we both finally must have fallen asleep, and in the morning the alarm woke us up before the sun rose. The bedroom light was still on, but it was getting hard to breathe again and the throbbing in my stomach had started back up.

I sat up in bed and covered my face with my hands – my elbows resting on my knees. Laci sat up next to me and began rubbing my back. I remembered how much better I had felt once I'd finally been able to pray last night. I took my hands off my face and turned and looked at Laci.

"Do you want to pray?" I asked her, and she nodded.

27

We got down on our knees and bowed our heads over the bed. I took Laci's hand and started to pray for her again.

"Dear Heavenly Father, please be with Laci and give her the strength to handle whatever lies ahead of us. Please keep her close to You and let her know how much You love her–"

A cry escaped from Laci and she sank to the floor, sobbing into her hands. I sat down next to her and wrapped my arms around her.

"Shhhhh," I soothed, holding her tightly with one arm and stroking her hair with the other. "Shhhhh."

Please don't let her feel like You've left her. Please let her know that You are here with her and will never leave her.

Laci started quieting down. She wiped her eyes and sat back.

"I'm sorry," she sniffed.

"It's okay," I whispered, brushing tears off her cheek.

Whatever happens today, please comfort her and see her through–

"You can keep praying," Laci said.

"I never stopped," I told her.

She leaned forward, resting her head against my shoulder while I continued.

"And I ask that You will hold her in Your arms, Lord, and give her Your peace. Amen."

Laci took a long, ragged breath and I could tell that she was feeling better too. She pressed her head tighter against me and she prayed.

She prayed for me just like I had prayed for her.

She didn't pray out loud like she usually did . . . but I know that's what she was doing.

I could feel it.

Once we got downstairs Laci couldn't eat breakfast, but I managed to eat some of the sausage and hash browns that Danica had been nice enough to make for us.

"Are you sure you don't want me to go with you?" Mike asked for the umpteenth time as I was draining the last of my orange juice.

"No," I said. "We're good."

"Okay," he nodded reluctantly.

In retrospect I should have let both Mike *and* Danica come along – it would have been better for Laci if I had. At that point, however, I didn't even want *Laci* there with me. I really wanted to be alone when I found out what the doctor had to say. But that, of course, wasn't even a remote possibility – Laci had barely let me out of her sight since we'd left Mexico City.

Dr. Keener again met us at the door to his office – unlocking it for us and giving us a small, evasive smile before leading us back into the same office that we'd first met him in the morning before. We sat down, Laci gripped my hand, and he began.

"I've assessed the results from all of testing that you've had done – both here and the tests that were done in Mexico. I found no evidence of anemia, depression, infection, diabetes, or kidney or liver disease. There was no indication of any vitamin deficiencies, thyroid abnormalities, or any problems with your heart or lungs. There were no biomarkers found in the cerebrospinal fluid that were definitive for diagnosis, and your genetic mapping showed no inherited diseases that would account for what we're seeing. There were also no signs of any brain tumors or any brain lesions – which is, of course, good. Blood flow to the brain doesn't seem to be compromised in any way, so we can rule that out as part of the problem as well."

No signs of any brain tumors.

I glanced at Laci, but didn't see a look of relief on her face — probably because she knew there was a "however" coming up.

"However," he said, "your MRI shows that the volume of gray matter in your brain is diminished ... particularly that of your hippocampus, which is responsible for learning and memory. The fact that you've been exhibiting mild cognitive impairment that can't be attributed to anything else, coupled with the results of the MRI, indicates a diagnosis of early-onset Alzheimer's disease."

"Mild cognitive impairment ..." I repeated, focusing on the beginning of his sentence instead of the end.

"Yes," he nodded.

"All those tests I did yesterday?"

"Your cognitive memory tests," he admitted, "were within normal limits."

"I did good on the tests," I clarified, "and you can't find anything wrong with me ..."

"Based upon the history you've provided," he glanced at Laci and then back at me, "I feel it's safe to say that we're witnessing a deficiency in your mental abilities that can't be attributed to anything else."

"So just because she says there's something wrong," I jabbed my finger at Laci, "you're diagnosing me with Alzheimer's?"

"You also indicated some concerns that you were apparently doing things and then not remembering them later, correct?"

I didn't answer.

"And," he reminded me, "the volume of your gray matter is diminished beyond what would be considered normal."

I still didn't say anything.

"And," he added, "the PET scan detected some metabolic abnormalities in your brain that would be consistent with what we would expect to find in a patient with Alzheimer's."

"But isn't there some kind of test you can do to know for sure?" Laci asked.

"Unfortunately, no," he answered, shaking his head. "The presence of certain markers can help confirm a diagnosis, but as I said, your husband doesn't have any of those markers at this time."

"At this time," I repeated.

He nodded. "Alzheimer's – particularly early-onset Alzheimer's – often has a genetic component, but it doesn't always. You have no genetic markers typical of Alzheimer's. The biomarkers found in the cerebrospinal fluid can also be used for diagnosis, but the absence of these markers doesn't mean that Alzheimer's can be ruled out. It wouldn't surprise me to find the appearance of those markers six months or a year down the road."

"Why did he do so good on the test he took yesterday though?" Laci asked. "Why does it come and go the way it does?"

"It's likely that certain parts of your husband's brain are compensating for the parts that are degenerating. It's as if one part shuts down and you see the symptoms exhibiting themselves in his behavior or in his abilities. Then, the brain finds new connections and accesses other parts of his brain that aren't damaged and his functions return to normal again. As *those* areas become affected, new connections to other undamaged areas have to be found and – until they are – you see the symptoms."

"How long does it take for the brain to find new connections?" Laci asked.

"I'm oversimplifying things," he said gently. "It's a little more complicated than I'm making it out to be, and no two cases are exactly alike, but overall, the amount of time it takes just depends on where the new connections need to go to and how many undamaged parts of the brain are left."

"And eventually there won't be any undamaged parts to connect to," I stated.

Dr. Keener looked back at me. "Nothing can repair the damage to the brain tissue once it's occurred," he admitted, "but there *are* treatments that can drastically slow down the progression of the disease – keeping as much tissue as possible undamaged for as long as possible."

"What kind of treatments?" Laci asked, swallowing hard.

"In my opinion, the most effective treatment right now is a medication called Coceptiva. It's only been on the market for about a year, but the initial results are very, very promising." Then he added, "There are also some clinical trials that you may want to consider."

"What are the side effects?" I asked.

"Of the clinical trials?"

"No," I said. "Of that medicine . . . Coceptiva?"

"Minimal," he said. "That's one of the reasons I'm recommending it. Dry mouth and rash are the most commonly reported complaints. Sometimes liver function can be compromised, but your liver enzymes are all within completely normal limits right now so I would just recommend having blood work done every three months to make sure those levels stay where they should."

"What about the clinical trials?" Laci asked.

"New drugs, combinations of drugs, and treatments are being developed all the time," he said. "All clinical trials are approved by the FDA, but that doesn't mean that they're necessarily safe or that they're effective. That's the main purpose of the trial – to determine if they're safe and if they're effective."

"Can I start taking this Coceptiva now and think about clinical trials later?"

"Certainly," Dr. Keener nodded. "Many patients who choose to get involved in clinical trials do so only after they've exhausted all traditional treatments that are available."

"I want to wait on that," I told Laci. Then to Dr. Keener I said, "Thank you," and I asked him to point us to the pharmacy.

The pharmacy was just across the street and as we walked to it, I felt strangely buoyed by Dr. Keener's words.

No signs of any brain tumors. No signs of any brain tumors.

"Any chance I can talk you into going to that pancake house we passed on the way over here?" I asked Laci after we'd picked up the prescription.

"You're hungry?"

I looked at Laci and thought about her question.

Ever since we'd left the doctor's office, my mind had been racing to remember what I'd read over the past few weeks about the symptoms of Alzheimer's.

Becoming confused in familiar places.

Dressing inappropriately for the weather.

Trouble handling money and paying bills.

Granted, it got worse . . .

Continuously repeating stories.

Increased memory loss and confusion.

Lack of concern for hygiene and appearance.

And worse . . .

Inability to communicate.

Lack of control of bowel and bladder.

Inability to recognize oneself or family.

But this was better than finding out that I was going to be dead in three to six months from brain tumor, wasn't it? And what had I read about the life expectancy of people diagnosed with Alzheimer's? *Five to twenty years from onset of symptoms?* Something like that. Certainly not three to six months . . . five to twenty *years*.

Laci was looking at me, waiting for an answer.

"Yeah," I nodded, giving her a little smile. "I'm hungry."

When we got to the restaurant the hostess showed us to a booth, and I let Laci sit down first, sliding in next to her. Our waitress showed up and took our drink orders and then we looked over our menus.

"I want you to *eat* something," I told Laci. She nodded reluctantly, and when the waitress returned she ordered some sort of fruit dish with oatmeal.

"Why would you come to a *pancake house* and order *oatmeal* when they've got all this other good stuff?" I asked her, sweeping my hand across the restaurant.

"I'm trying to eat healthy!" she argued.

"Do I still have to eat healthy?"

She looked at me for a moment as if she was trying to decide whether to cry or laugh.

"As if you've ever tried to eat healthy," she finally muttered. I smiled at her.

I took a sip of water and then reached across her and into her purse, pulling out the little bag with my new drug in it. I opened the bottle and dumped one out onto my hand. I held it up for her to see.

"The results have been *promising*," I reminded her, tipping the little blue pill back and forth. "Very, very promising."

She swallowed hard, nodded, and then watched me wash it down with some more water. I started looking at the pamphlet that had come along with it.

"Most common side effects," I read aloud, "include dry mouth, *foul-smelling urine*, and a localized rash *in the groin area?*"

Laci almost smiled.

"I think he failed to mention that part," I said wryly and then I went on. "*Potential* side effects NOT so commonly reported include nausea, constipation, upset stomach, shortness of breath, jaundice, dizziness, and/or fainting. Hallucinations have been reported in a small number of cases. Additionally, a small number of patients report experiencing thoughts of suicide. If you develop suicidal thoughts, contact your physician immediately. Contact your physician immediately if you notice an unusual increase in heart rate, if you develop an erratic heart rhythm, or if you notice yellowing of the skin and/or whites of the eyes or experience sudden blindness."

"Seriously?" I asked her, hoping for a real smile. "They think they need to *tell* me that I should contact my doctor immediately if I experience sudden blindness?"

"Maybe we should talk to Mike before you take any more of those," Laci said worriedly. "None of that sounds too good to me."

"Relax," I said, "none of that stuff is going to happen – except for probably the *groin rash* . . ."

I finally got the smile that I'd been hoping for. I reached into her purse again, this time pulling out the bottle of pain reliever that she'd been carrying around ever since she'd broken her shoulder four years earlier.

"Ever looked at *this?*" I asked, unfolding the warning label that was taped to the bottle. I started reading. "Heartburn, stomach bleeding, ulcers, high blood pressure . . ."

"It really says all that?" she asked, looking at the label with me. I nodded.

I could tell that she was still worried about me taking this new medicine though . . . and worried about me in general.

"If it'll make you feel better," I assured her, leaning over her one last time and throwing both of the bottles back into her purse, "I'll ask Mike what he thinks about it. If he feels at all like I shouldn't be taking it, I'll stop, okay?"

She nodded.

"*And,*" I added, "if I develop a groin rash, I promise I'll stop too."

When the waiter brought Laci her oatmeal and me my chocolate chip pancakes (with whipped cream and powdered sugar), we prayed again and then started eating.

"What are we going to tell people?" Laci asked after she'd taken about two bites of her oatmeal.

"What d'ya mean?"

"I mean . . . I mean – are we going to *tell* people about this or are we going to keep it to ourselves or . . ."

"Oh," I said, taking another slice at my pancakes with the side of my fork. "I don't know. I haven't really thought about it. What do you think?"

"Whatever you want to do."

"Well, we have to tell Mike and Danica," I said. "And Dorito . . ."

Laci nodded.

I thought for a moment.

"And I don't think it would be very fair to put Dorito in a position of keeping it a secret from his brother and sisters," I finally said, spearing some pancakes.

Laci nodded again.

"And so if the kids find out, you know Lily's gonna tell Jordan and that means that Charlotte and Mrs. White are going to find out . . ."

"And Tanner," Laci finished.

I nodded.

"I have to tell my dad," Laci added quietly. (Laci's dad lived down in Florida now.) I wondered silently if we needed to tell *my* dad.

"Maybe we should go *see* the kids," Laci suggested. "Tell them in person."

"I . . . I don't see how we can do that," I said, shaking my head. I didn't really want to give them news like this over the phone either, but they were all pretty spread out. Grace was in California and the other three girls were all here in the Midwest. But Dorito was in

Mexico of course, and Marco was all the way in *Australia*. There was no way we were going to be able to see each one of the kids in person before word spread like wildfire and they all found out from each other.

"No," she sighed. "I guess not."

I sighed too. There probably wasn't going to be a *right* way to tell everyone . . . or at least not a *good* way.

"Can we just eat right now and figure it out later?" I asked her. I was still holding my fork with an uneaten mouthful of pancakes on the end of it.

"I'm sorry," she said, looking teary-eyed.

I set my fork down and put my arm around her waist.

"Don't be sorry," I said, putting my other arm around her too and drawing her against me. "I just want you to eat something and stop worrying . . ."

"How am I supposed to stop worrying?" she asked in a choked voice.

I closed my eyes and burrowed my face into her hair.

"God hasn't given us the spirit of fear," I whispered in her ear, "but of power and love."

I surprised myself by doing this. Memorizing Scripture and spouting it off at appropriate times was *Laci's* specialty, not mine.

She immediately stopped crying and pulled back, turning to stare at me with a look of awe on her face. (I guess my quoting Scripture had surprised her, too.)

"Say the rest," she breathed.

"I, uhhhh . . . I don't know the rest," I admitted.

"God hasn't given us the spirit of fear," she repeated, "but of power, and of love, and of a *sound mind*."

I looked at her and then smiled. She smiled back. Then I kissed her and she kissed me back.

"You taste like syrup," she said.

"You should try it," I said, holding up my forkful of pancakes to her mouth. "I promise you it's a whole lot better than oatmeal."

She took the pancakes off the end of my fork and smiled at me again while she chewed. I silently thanked God for putting exactly the right piece of Scripture in my head at exactly the right moment . . . and then I asked Him to please let those little blue pills that were rattling around in the pharmacy bottle in Laci's purse start to do their stuff.

~ ~ ~

I WAS NOT at all surprised to find Mike and Danica waiting for us when we got back to their house. Danica looked at us worriedly and Mike expectantly as they ushered us into their living room and we all sat down.

I told them what Dr. Keener had said and I watched Danica tear up as Mike shook his head and turned away, unable to bring himself to look at me.

Danica came over to the couch where Laci and I were and sat down next to Laci, wrapping an arm around her and murmuring softly into her ear like she had the night before. Mike finally turned back to us and sat on the arm of the couch by me, putting his hand on my shoulder.

I'd been feeling pretty good until now. *No brain tumor . . . five to twenty years . . .*

But now I looked up at Mike and saw tears in his eyes too, and next to me all I heard was the sound of Laci sobbing.

And suddenly, I didn't feel too good anymore.

Within an hour, Danica claimed she needed to go shopping for something and Laci offered to go with her. I knew it was all a big ruse so that the two of them could have some time together and so Laci could cry some more and Danica could console her. But that was fine with me. I wanted the chance to talk with Mike when Laci wasn't around anyway.

39

"Lay it out for me, Mike," I said as soon as they'd left. "I wanna know exactly what's gonna happen."

"I don't *know* exactly what's gonna happen."

"You've got a pretty good idea."

"A lot can happen," he said. "It's different for everyone."

"Then tell me what *might* happen."

He sighed and looked away. After a minute he began.

"Every day," he said, looking back at me, "they're making advances . . . coming up with new treatments, new medications. This Coceptiva he's put you on? I've heard really great things about it."

"But nothing's going to stop it," I clarified.

"No," he admitted. "But it can really stave it off for months."

"Months?" *Only months?*

"Maybe years . . ."

"And then what?"

"And then . . . then it starts to lose its effectiveness."

"And?"

"And what?"

"And what happens then?"

"I told you," he said. "No one can predict these things – every person is different."

"Mike," I said, pleadingly. "*Talk* to me. Just tell me what's probably gonna happen."

He took a deep breath and finally nodded.

"One thing that often happens," he began, "is that your short-term memory will start to go. Your long-term memory may stay intact, but you won't be able to remember what happened *yesterday*. Simple things that used to be second nature to you will become more difficult . . . like how to dial a number on the phone, how to drive to the grocery store."

He didn't go on.

"And?" I pressed.

"After a while," he said finally, "you're going to have trouble doing things like brushing your teeth or feeding yourself. Eventually – well, eventually you won't remember how to do anything."

"How long before I'm like that?"

"There's no telling," he said. "It just depends on how aggressive it is."

"How will I die?"

"You could die from anything, Dave, just like the rest of us. Heart attack, stroke, cancer . . ."

"But what if none of that happens?"

"Your brain is slowly destroying itself," he said reluctantly, "and your body will just gradually shut down. A lot of times a decision is made not to go with a feeding tube or anything. Once the patient completely stops eating and drinking, they go pretty quickly."

"What's that gonna be like?"

"I don't think you're really going to be there. I think you'll already be – gone."

"But what about the guy who *is* there? What's it gonna feel like for him?"

"Don't worry about him, Dave," Mike said softly, looking me right in the eyes. "I promise you that we're going to take good care of him."

A little bit later – when Mike had excused himself to return a call to his office – I pulled out my laptop. Until today I'd had no idea what exactly had been wrong with me and so I had searched for information on an entire slew of things that might have been causing my symptoms. Now, however, I zeroed in on one thing – Alzheimer's disease – and I paid much closer attention to what I read.

Soon I learned that while it was indeed *possible* for someone to live for five to twenty years after being diagnosed with Alzheimer's, it certainly wasn't very likely. As a matter of fact, the average life expectancy for patients after they had been diagnosed was . . .

"Four and a half years?" I cried when Mike got off the phone.

He just looked at me and didn't say anything.

"Is that with or without the little blue pills?" I asked hotly.

"The medicine isn't going to prolong your life," he said softly. "It's going to make your quality of life better."

"What else are you keeping from me?"

"I'm not keeping anything from you!" he insisted. "You didn't ask me what the average life expectancy was."

"Four and a half years?" I asked again, hoarsely. "Is that really true? I've only got four and a half years?"

"No one can tell you exactly how long you're going to live," he said. "You know that."

He looked sad and I felt guilty for snapping at him.

"What *can* you tell me?" I asked quietly.

He hesitated for a moment, but eventually answered.

"In general," he said, "you can expect to live about half as long as you would if you didn't have Alzheimer's."

"Half as long," I repeated.

He nodded.

"So," I clarified, "in other words, if I was going to live for thirty more years, now I'm only gonna live for fifteen?"

"As a general rule of thumb," he said, nodding again.

"But the average is only four and a half years . . ."

"A lot of people who are diagnosed are a lot older than you are," he explained. "Plus your overall, general health plays a big role."

"So . . . so I probably have a lot of time left."

"Those aren't the only factors," he told me.

"What else?"

42

He hesitated. "How aggressive the disease is," he finally said. "It varies greatly from patient to patient. Sometimes it progresses quickly, sometimes slowly. There's a general feeling that the younger someone is when they're diagnosed, the more aggressive it tends to be, but," he hastened to add, "research hasn't really shown that that's necessarily true."

A month ago my biggest worry had been whether or not the gas grill was going to run out of propane before the burgers were done. Now, suddenly, I was likely to find myself an hour from home with no idea how I'd gotten there or that the contents of our kitchen drawers had mysteriously been relocated to my office.

Somehow that was feeling pretty aggressive.

I was quiet for a moment.

"Remember how you said that a lot of times they decide not to use a feeding tube and stuff?" I finally asked, breaking the silence.

He nodded.

"Who's gonna decide that?" I wanted to know. "Laci?"

He nodded again. "Most likely – unless you appoint someone else to be your health care power-of-attorney ahead of time."

"What if I have a living will?" I asked.

"Ultimately Laci would make the final decisions even if they go against what you've put into a living will."

"So what's the point in having one then?" I asked.

"Well, for one thing, so Laci will know exactly what you want."

"Why can't I just *tell* her what I want?"

"When people are having to make difficult choices, it's a lot easier for them to make a rational decision if it's documented ahead of time. Plus, it'll be a lot harder for anyone to fight her decisions if she has proof that she's following your wishes."

"You mean, like if the kids want her to do something different?"

"Well, yeah," he agreed, "but I was really thinking of the doctors. Medical professionals are always afraid of lawsuits and *not* treating somebody is a surefire way of getting into trouble. If you have an advanced directive and Laci's going along with it, she probably won't have any problems."

"Will you help me make one?"

"Sure."

"Tonight?"

"*Tonight?* I don't think we need to—"

"I know exactly what I want and I wanna write it down tonight," I said emphatically.

"Okay," Mike said slowly. "We'll do it tonight."

Before Laci and Danica got back, I called Dorito. He answered the phone before I even heard it ring.

"Hi, Dad," he said, trying unsuccessfully to sound calm.

"Hey, Dorito. How's everything going down there?"

"What did the doctor say?"

"He, ummm, he won't be able to tell us anything until tomorrow."

"Tomorrow?!" Dorito cried. "I thought Mom said you were going to find out this morning!"

"Well, I guess some of the test results aren't back yet."

He sighed heavily. "How are you doing?" he asked in a resigned voice.

"Great," I said. "I'm doing great. Go back to work and quit worrying about me. I'm fine. I'll talk to you tomorrow."

I hung up the phone and turned around to find Mike standing in the doorway and looking at me.

"I . . . I just can't tell him right now," I said apologetically.

He nodded slightly, blinked away a fresh set of tears, and left the room.

44

That evening, Laci and I sat down with Mike and Danica at their dining room table and worked on my living will. Mike was very thorough, and you could tell he was really making sure that he was covering all the bases. It took a lot longer than I had figured it would and we'd already been at it for over an hour when Mike asked, "Okay. What if you get to the point where you can't swallow your food? Do you want a feeding tube?"

"No," I said.

"Yes!" Laci argued. "I'm not gonna just let you waste away!"

"No!" I said again. "If somebody needs to feed me or whatever, I guess that's fine, but if I can't even *swallow* by myself you need to let me go."

Laci sighed in resignation.

"What if you get cancer?" Mike asked.

"Just let it go," I said.

"So, you're just not even going to *try* to have a good life?" Laci asked, exasperated. "If next week you get diagnosed with cancer or something you're just gonna curl up into a ball and die?"

"If I get diagnosed with cancer next week I hope I can still make my own decisions," I told her. "We're not talking about *next week* . . . we're talking about what I want after I can't speak for myself anymore. And if I'm not myself and I can't decide what I want any more, then yes . . . I'd just as soon go ahead and die."

"Fine," Laci said, crossing her arms. She'd lost just about every argument we'd had since we started.

"Oxygen?" Mike asked.

"No."

Laci didn't even say anything.

"Actually," Danica said quietly, "it's more of a comfort measure than anything else. It's not really going to prolong your life once it's time."

"Okay, fine." I looked at Laci. "You can give me oxygen."

"Whoop-dee-do," Laci answered.

"That pretty much covers everything," Mike said, gathering the papers up and straightening the stack. "Just take this to your lawyer's office and have them write it up. I'll be glad to double-check it when it's ready."

"Thank you, Mike," Laci told him.

"Wait a minute," I said. "I'm not done. We haven't talked about me going into a nursing home."

"That's not really something you'd specifically stipulate in a living will," Mike said.

"Well, I think we should talk about it anyway."

"Okay."

I turned to Laci.

"As soon as I get bad I want you to put me into a nursing home."

"No!"

"Yes."

"Absolutely not!" Laci said, setting her jaw. "I am *never* going to put you in a nursing home!"

"Laci, that's what I want."

"Well, you know what?" she yelled. "I don't really *care* what you want anymore! I'm the one who's going to be in charge and I can pretty much guarantee you that I will not be putting you into a nursing home!"

"Well then," I said. "I'll just appoint somebody else to be my power-of-attorney . . . somebody who'll do what I want."

"You can't do that!" she cried.

"Yes, I can, can't I?"

I glanced over at Mike, who was clearly not comfortable being in the middle of this.

"Actually," he told her gently, "he can."

Laci's mouth dropped open in dismay and she glanced at Danica, obviously hoping that she was going to argue with Mike. When that didn't happen, Laci slammed her hand against the table, got up from her chair, stormed through the living room, and slammed the front door on her way out. Danica stood up and followed after her.

Mike and I didn't say anything for a while.

"She's so stubborn," I finally said.

"And you're not?"

"It's *my* life, Mike."

"It's not just *your* life," he said. "What if Laci was the one who was sick? Think about how this would be affecting you."

"I know how this is affecting her! I'm trying to make things as easy for her as I can!"

"Look," he said, "I know you don't want to be a burden on her, but I personally think that she should get to be a part of this decision . . . if you ask my opinion."

"Which I didn't."

"Okay," he said, standing up. "I've created enough chaos for one night. I'm going to bed."

"It's not your fault," I said quietly.

"I know."

"And I'll talk to her."

"I know."

Danica came back into the house alone a few minutes later and I looked at her expectantly.

"She just wanted to be alone for a bit," she explained quietly.

I nodded but put on my jacket and went outside into the cold night air. I went down to the end of the driveway and looked up and down the street, but couldn't see Laci anywhere. Mike and Danica lived in a sprawling neighborhood and I knew I had little hope of finding her, so I went back to their front porch and sat down to wait.

I was still sitting there twenty minutes later when Laci finally came back. She was only wearing jeans and a sweater and she had her arms wrapped around her body, trying to ward off the cold. She stopped when she saw me and didn't move until I held my hand out to her.

"Come here," I said softly. She walked over to me, took my hand and let me pull her down next to me.

Taking my jacket off, I put it over her shoulders and then wrapped an arm around her. She leaned her head against me.

"Please don't make somebody else your power-of-attorney," she whispered against my neck. "Don't do that to me."

"I won't," I said. "You can do whatever you want. I guess I won't know the difference anyway."

"I . . . I'll go along with all the other things we talked about," she promised, sitting back and looking at me, "but I don't want to put you into a nursing home."

"Will you at least get somebody in to help you?" I asked.

"What do you mean?"

"Someone to stay with me so you can go out and stuff? Somebody who can handle me if it gets to where I can't walk or whatever?"

"I hadn't thought about that," she said. "That might be all right, I guess."

"You should have plenty of money to pay for somebody," I told her, "especially with that insurance we have . . ."

"Okay," she agreed. "I'll get some help as soon as I think I need it."

"No," I said. "I know you. I want you to get some help *before* you think you need it."

~ ~ ~

THE NEXT MORNING, Mike suggested that we take a walk. He waited until we were about two blocks from the house before he told me what was on his mind.

"We need to talk about Laci," he said.

I didn't say anything.

"This is going to be the hardest on her," he said hesitantly.

"You think I don't know that?"

He shut up and we trudged along.

"Sorry," I finally said.

"It's okay," he assured me.

"I'm just really worried about her."

"I know you are," he nodded, "but that's what I wanted to talk to you about. There are some things you're going to be able to do that can make this easier on her."

"Like what?"

"Well, like if you would stop driving."

"Stop driving?!"

"Yeah," Mike said. "I think that if you would voluntarily give up—"

"I drive just fine!"

"I . . . I know," he said, "but under the circumstances, it really isn't a good idea."

"I haven't had one problem!" I cried. "Not one accident, no tickets, nothing!"

"So you're going to wait until you *do* have a problem before you quit driving?" he asked. "Gonna wait until you kill somebody?"

"I'm not gonna kill anybody!" I insisted.

"Believe it or not," he said, "this is one of the hardest things I've ever seen people go through. When somebody insists on continuing to drive and then the husband or wife or a child has to either worry constantly or go through the process of forcing someone to give up their license . . ."

I didn't say anything.

"You know, last night you were telling her to stick you in a nursing home because you want to make things easy on her . . . well, if you really want to make things easy on her you'll give up driving before she has to *make* you give up driving."

"I drive just fine," I said again, quietly, but then I added, "but I'll think about it."

"There's something else I wanted to talk to you about . . ."

"What?"

"I think anybody in your circumstance," he said carefully, "is going to wonder at some point if it wouldn't be better if they were already dead. One day you might think that maybe the best thing for you to do would be to just end it all . . . to let Laci get on with her life."

I stopped walking and looked at him. *A small number of patients report experiencing thoughts of suicide . . . if you develop suicidal thoughts, contact your physician immediately . . .*

"What are you saying?" I asked.

He looked back at me for a long moment.

"I can see how you might think that you'd be doing her a big favor or something," he finally said, shaking his head, "but . . . well, if you were to do something like that then you might as well just kill Laci too."

"And here I thought you were going to offer to help."

"No," he said, shaking his head. "Absolutely not."

We looked at each other for a moment.

"I'm so worried about her," I finally said, my voice a strangled whisper.

50

"I know you are," he acknowledged, putting a hand on my shoulder. "And I know it's gonna be hard for her to take care of you and for her to watch you go through this and everything, but she's got a lot of people who are willing to support her and she *will* get through this . . . she *will* be alright."

I shook my head and looked away.

"She will be, David," he assured me. "Unless you do something stupid like kill yourself." He paused before he finished his thought. "If you do that?" he finally said, "well, I can promise you that she'll never get over it."

It was time to leave. We were all in the foyer and our bags were in the trunk of the car.

"Listen," Mike said. "Can we . . ."

He hesitated.

"What?" I asked.

"Danica and I would like to pray for you."

I didn't say anything, but Laci nodded and started crying again so we went into the living room and they put their hands on both of us and I closed my eyes – I honestly don't know if I'd ever felt so uncomfortable before in my entire life.

But then they prayed for me . . . *and* they prayed for Laci. And after that I felt better.

By the time they were finished I felt peace (which I guess made sense, since that's mostly what they had been praying for). I opened my eyes and looked at Laci. She still had tears in her eyes, but she wasn't crying anymore and I could tell that she felt it too.

"That medicine's gonna help," Mike told us in the driveway. "I think you'll be surprised."

I nodded at him, we all hugged each other goodbye, and Laci and I promised to call them if we needed anything.

Then I handed Laci the keys and told her she could drive.

~ ~ ~

IT WAS A four-hour trip back to Cavendish and we stopped and ate lunch along the way, so by the time we got to my sister Jessica's house, it was almost five o'clock.

Jessica knew we were back in the States. She knew I was having some tests done at the Mayo Clinic. She didn't know any specifics.

When we arrived, she was home alone – her husband, Chris, was still at work. She hugged us as we stepped into the living room, invited us to sit down, and didn't ask us any questions.

"Can I get you guys anything?" she asked. Laci and I both shook our heads. I could tell that Jess was dying to know what was going on, but she kept quiet.

"How's Dad doing?" I asked.

"About the same."

The same. That meant recognizing me and Jessica only about half the time, Laci rarely, and the grandkids and great-grandkids never.

I continued with the small talk, asking her about my nephew, CJ, my niece, Cassidy, and their families.

Great.

Everybody was just great.

"Any activity on the house?" I finally asked. (After it had become apparent that Dad wasn't going to even come close to a full recovery from his stroke, Jess and I had made the difficult decision to move him into a nursing home – excuse me . . . *long-term care facility*. We'd put his house on the market, but it wasn't in the greatest shape in the world and the real estate market was in a slump. It had been on the market for eight months already with no offers yet.)

"No," Jessica said, shaking her head, "but we're hoping that it'll start showing more this spring."

"Is it okay if we stay there for a few days?" I asked.

"Of course it is – or you can stay here if you want. Whatever works best for you guys."

I glanced at Laci.

"I . . . I think we'll probably stay there," I said finally, and Laci nodded. We needed time alone . . . to think, to decide what we were going to do.

"Okay," Jess answered. Nobody said anything for a moment and Jessica looked at me expectantly. I finally decided I'd better just tell her and get it over with.

And so I did.

~ ~ ~

TELLING JESS WAS just the beginning. After we got to my dad's house we started calling the kids and telling them – one by one.

It was . . . awful.

Really, really *awful*.

The first phone call we made was to Dorito since he was already waiting to find out what was going on anyway. He had spent even more time than I had online, figuring out what we might be facing, so he had a good idea exactly what a diagnosis of Alzheimer's meant and he was pretty upset.

Then we called the four girls, all of whom were doubly distressed – not only because of the diagnosis, but because they were hit with the news completely out of the blue. Apparently neither Laci nor Dorito had hinted to any of them what was going on.

We saved Marco for last since he was in Australia, where it was fairly early in the morning. There was quite a long bit of silence when I broke it to him.

"I'm going to come home," he finally said.

"For what?"

"To be with you!" he exclaimed. "To help you!"

"Help me what?" I asked.

He didn't say anything.

"Marco," I insisted, "everything's fine right now. There's no need for you to come home."

"I *want* to come home," he said quietly.

"Well, I *don't* want you to come home," I persisted. "You've worked way too hard to get where you are."

Marco was in the graduate program in Melbourne's School of Engineering.

Out of all of our kids, only Marco had followed me into engineering. Actually, however, he was becoming such a completely different type of engineer from what I was that I wasn't really sure if it even counted as "following me" or not.

Marco was studying to be a neuroprosthetic engineer – someone who designed and developed neural prostheses. Essentially, he wanted to make robotic devices that were actually hooked up to the nervous and muscular systems to replace missing or damaged body parts. Think about an amputee who has lost a foot. A neural prosthetic would replace the missing foot and actually respond just like a real foot would – the user wouldn't even need to think about what he or she was doing in order to walk naturally because the artificial limb would be sending and receiving signals just like a real foot would.

At first Marco had been fascinated with improving and refining the input coming in to the brain from prosthetic limbs (in other words, if you were touching something hot you would *know* you were touching something hot because you could actually feel it). But early in his freshman year, one of his lab professors had talked with him about the field of optical prosthetics, and after that he had been completely hooked. ("It's just like what Lily's got," he'd explained when he'd told us about it, "except that it's for your eyes.")

Our daughter Lily had been born completely deaf, but when she was little she'd gotten cochlear implants. Now, basically, Marco wanted to help blind people see as well as Lily could hear.

"I thought you were going to work on artificial *hands*," Grace had reminded him scornfully when he'd shared his change in plans with us. (His older sister by only a few months, Grace made it her personal mission in life to try and provoke Marco whenever she could.)

"Naw," he had said, waving his own hand at her. "Hands are overrated."

Now he was forever regaling us with talk of vitreous, phosphenes, and photodiodes. And so (even though technically Marco was going into engineering like I had), it was a whole lot easier for me to have a work-related conversation with Dorito, who had become an architect. When Marco talked about his future profession, he tended to leave the rest of us in the dust.

Marco had gotten his bachelor's degree from Princeton and had flown overseas only six months earlier once he'd gotten into the University of Melbourne. And now he was talking about coming home and throwing it all away?

"I want to come home," he said again, and I could tell that he was trying very hard not to cry.

"Marco," I insisted, "listen to me. You're coming home for the wedding in just a few months." (Grace was getting married during the summer.) "See how things are then, okay? If you get here and you decide you want to stay home then you can, but *please* finish out the semester. Please promise me that you won't let this stop you."

He didn't answer me.

"Marco?"

Still no answer.

"Marco?"

"What?" he finally asked.

"What you're doing makes me so proud," I said quietly. "Don't quit now, just because of this."

With that I heard him start to cry in earnest, and I looked up at Laci and shook my head.

"Here," she said quietly, reaching for the phone. "Let me talk to him."

I handed her the phone and walked into the kitchen as Laci quietly tried to reassure him. I peered out into the dark backyard and then went out onto the deck, into the cold night air.

Why?

Why, why, why, why, WHY?

I usually tried very hard not to ask that question – I really did – but I couldn't help myself right now. How could God *not* see what a huge mistake this was?

I propped my elbows on the deck rail and rested my face in my hands. I was still standing there like that a few minutes later when I heard the door open and Laci joined me. She put her hand on my back.

"Is he okay?" I asked, not lifting my head.

"He will be," she said quietly. She moved closer and wrapped an arm around me. I didn't move much except to press myself against her. We stood there like that, together, for a long time.

"I can't do this anymore tonight," I finally said, raising my head to look at her and she nodded understandingly. Next we had planned on calling Tanner and Charlotte and Mrs. White and Laci's dad, but I just couldn't take anymore right now.

"We'll do it tomorrow," Laci agreed quietly, and I nodded.

We went back into the house and turned on the television, not really paying attention to what was on. We ordered a pizza even though neither of us was particularly hungry and we only picked at it when it arrived.

After receiving my diagnosis, we'd both had a restless night and today the phone calls to the kids had left us completely drained. We wound up going to bed before nine o'clock and it seemed as though my head had barely hit the pillow before I was in a sound and dreamless sleep.

In the morning, when I woke up, it was light outside. I checked my watch and saw that it was seven o'clock. Turning my head quietly – in case she was still asleep – I looked toward Laci.

She was wide awake, staring at the ceiling.

She glanced over at me.

"Good morning," she said.

"Good morning."

"Did you sleep?" she asked.

"I don't think I moved all night," I answered. "Did you get any sleep?"

"I think so," she nodded.

"I'm going to call all the kids again today," I told her. "I think now that they've had a chance to let it sink in it might be good if I could just talk to them a little bit and let them know that I'm doing okay . . ."

"I think that's a good idea," Laci said, turning toward me.

After a moment, Laci got out of bed and pulled a pair of jeans on under her nightgown.

"What are you doing?"

"Going to the grocery store," she said, digging through her suitcase for a clean sweatshirt. "We don't have anything for breakfast."

She headed into the bathroom, carrying the sweatshirt with her.

I lay back in bed and was staring up at the ceiling – thinking about all the phone calls we'd made – when I suddenly remembered the afternoon that my father had called to tell me that my mother was gone.

They had been planning for their retirement for years. Shortly after I'd graduated from college, Mom and Dad had bought nineteen acres out in the country – about twelve miles from the city limits of Cavendish. Dad bought a four-wheeler and they'd had a pond dug. They went out there almost every weekend and fished and hunted and played.

When she was two years away from early retirement, Mom started working with an architect to design their "dream home." Dad contracted all the work out himself, supervising everything personally. They'd had the yard graded, but not landscaped because that was something they decided they wanted to do themselves after they moved in. Likewise, they'd had hardwoods put down in most of the rooms, but had left the floor in the kitchen unfinished (and the countertops, too) because Dad wanted to try his hand at tiling. Mom enjoyed painting, so they'd only had the walls primed, deciding they would pick their colors after they'd been in the house for a while.

Once everything was as complete as they'd planned to get it, they'd moved in. That was in April – the spring before my mom retired. The next month during graduation (at the high school where she had taught for over thirty years) they had honored my mother by letting her hand out all the diplomas to the graduating seniors.

By the middle of June, my mom had painted one of the guest bedrooms (she had gone with a mossy-green color) and had started papering the kitchen. Deciding to tackle the front yard, she'd ordered a truckload of fieldstone so that she could build some flower beds on either side of the front steps.

Dad hadn't planned on retiring until the end of the year, so he was at work the morning the stones were supposed to be delivered. When the truck arrived, the workers found Mom slumped in a chair on the front porch, and by the time Dad got to the hospital, she was gone . . . the victim of a pulmonary embolism.

She'd been retired for exactly three weeks.

That had been a hard phone call to get . . . and now I knew that it had been a hard phone call for my dad to *make*. Funny how I'd never thought about that until now.

Laci came out of the bathroom, disturbing my thoughts. She had her sweatshirt on now and was pulling her hair into a ponytail.

"Get up!" she said when she saw that I was still in bed.

"Why?"

"Because – I told you we need to go to the grocery store."

"Why do I have to go?"

She stopped winding the ponytail holder around her hair and stared at me.

"I . . . I just think we should both go," she said hesitantly.

"I'll be fine here by myself," I told her.

"I know," she stammered. "That's not it . . ."

"What is it then?" I asked.

She stared at me for another moment and then finally said, "Are you sure you'll be alright?"

"I'll be fine," I promised. "I'll wash some dishes while you're gone." (Last night she'd dropped a plate when she'd pulled it down from the cupboard and discovered a dead spider lying on top of it.)

She hesitated for another moment, but then finally agreed and – giving her hair a final twist – walked over to me and kissed me on the cheek. "I love you."

"I love you, too," I said, and then, when she didn't move, I told her, "I'll be fine. Now go."

She gave me one last reluctant look and finally left. When I heard the car pull out of the driveway, I reached over to the nightstand and picked up my phone.

I called Tanner, knowing that he was teaching and wouldn't answer, but I left what I hoped was a nonchalant message on his voicemail, asking him to give me a call when he had the chance. After that, I swung my legs out of bed and then made my way downstairs.

When I reached the kitchen I flipped on the light, surveyed the room, and sighed.

What a disaster . . . no wonder the house hadn't sold yet.

After Mom had died, Dad had decided not to retire. I think the idea of spending his days alone in the house that he and Mom had worked so hard on was more than he could bear. Apparently he also couldn't muster up enough energy or desire to complete any of the projects the two of them had started but never finished.

After Mom's funeral, Laci and the kids had gone back to Mexico, but I had stayed around for a few weeks to try to help out.

Eventually, of course, I'd needed to get back to work and to my family, but – before I left – Chris and Jessica and I had all tried to get him motivated to fix stuff up.

Jessica had offered to paint, but Dad claimed he didn't know what colors he wanted to go with. The lawn never got seeded so weeds grew up instead (and in the years that followed he mowed them down only about once a month if Chris didn't come over and do it for him first). I said I'd pay someone to tile the kitchen floor, but Dad insisted that he was going to do it himself, and one day he bought some cheap vinyl flooring and put that down instead.

Once it had become obvious that he wasn't going to take care of the place, we had gently suggested that he might want to consider moving into something that didn't require quite as much upkeep, but he wouldn't hear of it, and things had been going steadily downhill ever since.

Now – as I stood staring into the kitchen – I noticed that the vinyl flooring was loose and curling on the edges where it met the hardwood floor of the dining room. Three boxes of ceramic tile were stacked in front of the cupboards to the right of the fridge (the countertops were still just bare particle board). I took down some plates and bowls from the cupboard to wash and thought I saw a mouse dropping in one of the bowls. I decided not to look too closely, sighed again, and turned the faucet on.

I had cleaned only one cup when the doorbell rang. I dried my hands, threw the dishtowel over my shoulder, and walked into the living room. Then I opened the front door and looked onto the porch . . . it was Mrs. White.

Like my dad, Mrs. White had also moved into an assisted living facility about a year earlier. Hers, however, was quite different from the place where my dad lived. At Mrs. White's, there were several levels of care available, including one for people who (like my dad) needed constant supervision. But there was also an independent-living section. This is where Mrs. White lived and she was provided with one meal each day in the main dining room, light housekeeping once a week (including fresh linens) and little call buttons throughout her apartment that she could push if she ever had any trouble. She cooked almost every day, walked for at least an hour when the weather was nice, and drove herself to the YMCA three times a week to do water aerobics and use the exercise machines. She also still drove five hours at least once a month to visit Charlotte and Jordan in Chicago and she had a cat and two finches (which, personally, I thought was a poor combination).

When I saw Mrs. White's face, I could tell immediately that she already knew.

"Hi," I said, trying to smile at her.

"Hi, honey," she answered as she gave me a long, tight hug. "How are you doing?"

"Lovely."

"I'm so sorry," she whispered, rubbing my back. I nodded against her.

"Who told you?" I asked when we pulled apart from one another. "Jess?"

"No," she answered, shaking her head. "Charlotte called me about ten o'clock last night."

I *knew* Lily was going to call Jordan. I closed my eyes at the thought of Charlotte finding out.

"Can I come in?"

"Oh!" I said, opening my eyes and stepping aside. "Sorry."

"Am I catching you at a bad time?" she asked, eying the dish towel.

"No," I said, following behind her. "I was just trying to clean up a bit."

"Ahhhh," she said knowingly.

We sat down on the couch.

"How . . . how's Charlotte doing with it?" I asked.

"About like you'd expect." (Which meant not good.)

"I'm sorry," I said, shaking my head. "I was going to call both of you today."

"It's alright," Mrs. White assured me, then, "How are *you* doing with it?" She spoke gently, putting her hand on top of mine.

"I don't know," I said, shaking my head again. I gave her a small shrug.

She gave me another knowing look.

"Where's Laci?" she asked after a moment.

"Grocery store."

Mrs. White nodded.

"How's she handling it?"

I started to answer, but couldn't. Instead I covered my eyes with my hand and shook my head one last time. Mrs. White put her arm around me and pulled me close and I felt the tears coming.

Resting against Mrs. White like that, being comforted by her, was familiar to me, and I let her hold me for a minute.

But then my phone rang and I pulled away, wiping my eyes so that I could see the screen.

"It's Tanner," I said. She nodded at me and I took a deep breath before I answered it.

"Hi," I said, managing to sound (in my opinion) fairly normal.

"What's up?" he asked. I could tell just by the tone of his voice that he didn't already know.

"I wondered if you wanted to grab a bite to eat tonight?" I asked, standing up and beginning to pace around the living room.

"You're in town?"

"Yep."

"I thought you guys weren't gonna be back until summer . . ."

"We had some stuff to take care of," I explained vaguely, glancing at Mrs. White.

"Is your dad okay?"

"Yeah . . . well, you know. About the same."

"I saw him a few days ago," Tanner said.

"You did?" I asked. "Where?"

"At the *nur-sing home?*" Tanner suggested slowly as if he were speaking to a demented three-year-old.

"You went to see my dad at the nursing home?"

"No," he said wryly. "I went to the nursing home to grab some puréed steak. I just happened to see your dad while I was there."

He visited my dad at the nursing home . . .

I closed my eyes again.

"So do you want to have dinner tonight," I finally asked, "or are you already busy?"

"Let's see," he said, more to himself than to me. "The girls play at home tonight and the JV game starts at six . . . but as long as everybody shows up like they're supposed to I can probably get away by six-thirty or so. Then if I could get back by eight-thirty or nine to make sure everything gets locked up and the refs get paid . . . Yeah, that'll work alright."

"You sure?"

"Yeah, I'm sure," he said. "Where ya wanna meet?"

"I don't care."

"There's this new Italian-American place across from the Y, where the bowling alley used to be . . . wanna try there?"

"Sure," I agreed. "I'll meet you there a little after six-thirty."

We hung up and Mrs. White and I looked at each other.

"This is going to be another great day," I told her.

She looked at me understandingly.

"Are you doing anything for dinner tonight?" I asked.

"You don't want me there," she said, shaking her head.

"No," I agreed. "But I was thinking it would really be good for Laci if you two spent some time together."

"I'd love to have dinner with her," she nodded.

"Thanks." I looked at Mrs. White for a moment and then said, in almost a whisper, "I'm so worried about her."

"I know you are."

"This is going to be so hard on her."

"God is going to take care of her, David," she said softly. "You have to believe that."

"I don't want her to have to go through this," I said, my voice breaking.

She put her hand on mine again and looked into my eyes. "He's not going to give her anything that she can't handle."

"I don't want her to have to *handle* anything!"

"He loves her even more than you do," she reminded me gently.

I looked away, not really wanting to cry again.

"I made a living will," I finally said after a long while, changing the subject slightly.

"That's good," Mrs. White nodded.

"And I'm going to make a file for her of all the things she needs to know about our accounts and stuff. Everything's pretty automated," I went on, "but she doesn't even know where half our money is or what bills we pay every month or anything. I always take care of all that kind of stuff."

"That's a good idea," she agreed.

"She's finally going to have to learn to use a computer."

Mrs. White smiled.

"I'm just . . . I'm just going to try and do whatever I can to make things as easy for her as possible."

She nodded again.

"I told her I wanted to go into a nursing home as soon as I started to get bad," I went on, "but she threw a fit."

"You what?"

66

"I told her I wanted to go into a nursing home as soon as–"

"A nursing home?" Mrs. White interrupted. "You honestly thought that somehow you were going to be able to talk Laci into putting you into a nursing home?"

"What's wrong with a nursing home?" I asked defensively. "*You're* the one who talked me into convincing Jessica that we should put Dad into a nursing home!"

"I know," she answered.

"And you're practically living in one yourself!"

"I know," she said again, patiently.

"So why can't I go into one?"

She looked at me incredulously for a moment.

"Do you even *know* Laci?" she finally asked. I had a feeling it was a rhetorical question, so I didn't answer.

"What has she spent her whole life doing?" she went on.

"Uhhh . . . working at the orphanage?"

"No," Mrs. White said. "Her *whole* life. What has her *whole life* been about?"

"Uhhh . . ." I tried again. "God?"

She rolled her eyes at me.

"Honestly," she muttered, "how can someone as smart as you are be so stupid?"

I figured this was another rhetorical question.

"Yes, God," she went on, "but that's not what I'm talking about. What makes Laci happier than anything else in the world?"

Not the orphanage . . . not God . . .

She rolled her eyes at me a second time and shook her head, giving me a look that was full of something between disbelief and disgust.

"It's not rocket science, David . . . it's *Laci.*" She stared at me earnestly and then finally said quietly, "Hasn't Laci's whole life been about helping other people?"

Oh.

I nodded slowly.

"And so," she continued, "instead of putting you into a nursing home and letting *other* people take care of you, doesn't it stand to reason that Laci would want to be the one to take care of you herself?"

I nodded a little more emphatically. That actually did make a whole lot of sense.

We heard the front door open and Mrs. White looked at me intently. Then she gave my hand a squeeze.

"And you need to let her," she added quietly. She patted my hand and then went to greet Laci at the front door.

Getting up off the couch, I followed after her, taking both of the bags from Laci that she was carrying (so that she and Mrs. White could hug each other). Then I carried the bags into the kitchen (so that I wouldn't have to see Laci's eyes filling with tears as Mrs. White whispered words of encouragement to her).

Setting them down on the counter, I started unloading the groceries. The first thing I pulled out of one of the bags was a package of powdered sugar mini-doughnuts (my favorite) and immediately after that I found a six-pack of Coke in glass bottles (another favorite).

I couldn't help but smile. Both of these things were – in Laci's opinion – all but toxic. It went against every fiber of her being to buy them for me, but (just like Mrs. White had said) Laci wanted nothing more than to help other people.

It might seem paradoxical to think that her buying me something she considered practically poisonous could be considered "helping" me, but I knew that Laci wasn't worried about my nutritional intake right now. Laci just wanted to see me smile.

I tried to remember the last time that I had smiled and I realized immediately that it had been two days earlier – at the pancake house in Rochester.

Although I'd just been diagnosed with Alzheimer's less than an hour before, I had been in a surprisingly good mood at that point because I was still feeling pretty happy to know that I didn't have brain cancer. While we'd been waiting for our food, I'd joked around with Laci about the side effects of my new medicine (and had even gotten a smile from her, too).

But after that, my mood had gone downhill rather quickly once we'd gotten back to Mike and Danica's and I'd seen how upset they were about my diagnosis. And the next day we'd had to tell Jessica and the kids about it and that, of course, had only made things worse. I definitely hadn't smiled since my joke about groin rashes at the restaurant.

And, I realized, Laci hadn't smiled since then either.

I looked at the doughnuts again and was suddenly struck with a thought.

I wonder . . .

I heard Laci and Mrs. White coming into the kitchen, and I glanced at the doughnuts one more time.

Was it really that simple?

"Would you like to have some breakfast with us?" Laci was offering to Mrs. White as they reached the kitchen.

"Well . . ." she hedged.

"I've got plenty of food," Laci assured her. "I bought cereal and bagels and bacon and eggs and dough—"

"And that's it," I interrupted, snatching the doughnuts off the counter and hiding them behind my back.

Laci looked at me, surprised.

"That's it," I said again, ignoring Laci's stare and looking at Mrs. White. "We've got cereal and bagels and bacon and eggs and if you don't like any of that then you can go to McDonald's and get something."

"David!" Laci cried.

"What?" I asked innocently.

"You are not going to eat all sixteen of those by yourself!"

"All sixteen of what?"

She put one hand on her hip and held out her other one. "Give those here!"

"I don't have anything," I said, backing away. With my free hand I grabbed the Coke and pulled that behind my back too.

"David!" she cried again.

"What?" I asked again.

"You have to share those!"

"No, I don't!"

"David!" Laci scolded. "Give Mrs. White a doughnut!"

"I don't have any doughnuts," I insisted, taking another step away from her. I was backed up against the counter when Mrs. White's phone rang.

"It's okay," she assured Laci, looking at her phone. "I really don't need any doughnuts."

"There," I said, as Mrs. White stepped into the living room to answer her call. "She doesn't want any anyway."

"I didn't buy them just for you!"

"Yes, you did," I smiled, taking a step toward her. She looked at me, perplexed, and I went on. "You bought them for me because you love me."

She opened her mouth as if to say something, but then closed it again. She appeared to be taken aback.

"And," I continued, stepping even closer and putting my arms around her waist, "you wanted to make me happy."

I think she was completely baffled by the way I was acting, but when I lowered my lips to hers she let me kiss them. I squeezed her gently because I was still holding the doughnuts and the Coke and when I pulled away I smiled at her again.

"Did it make you happy?" she finally asked.

"You always make me happy," I told her softly, and she gave me the first smile I'd seen in two days.

70

I gave her another kiss, longer this time, and when I was done Laci said, "I'll be sure to keep doughnuts in stock."

"And Coke," I reminded her.

"Right," she nodded. "And Coke."

Mrs. White came back into the kitchen and Laci and I let go of each another. I set the doughnuts and the Coke on the counter.

"Would you like a doughnut?" I offered Mrs. White, opening the package.

"I wouldn't want to risk losing a limb."

"I'm suddenly feeling very generous," I promised, pushing them toward her.

She looked at me suspiciously, but then reached in and took a doughnut. "That was Jordan," she said, nodding to her phone.

"Oh."

"They're going to come visit this weekend," she explained.

"Oh," I said again, nodding. I wasn't smiling anymore.

"Charlotte's going to be okay," Mrs. White promised quietly, putting a hand on my shoulder. I looked at her skeptically. "I know it's not going to be easy at first, but you and I both know that she *will* manage to get through this."

I gave her another nod, but I felt myself sigh.

"I think," I said, glancing at Laci, "that we're going to need more doughnuts."

We had bacon and eggs with our doughnuts and Coke. Laci claimed that the entire combination was disgusting, but I noticed that didn't stop her from eating *four* of my doughnuts (compared to Mrs. White's three), leaving me with only nine. We didn't talk about Charlotte or Alzheimer's or my dad, but instead kept the conversation on fun stuff (like grandkids) and we smiled and kidded and laughed.

71

The more I smiled and the more I laughed, the more Laci did too. It was almost amazing to watch how she mirrored whatever she saw in me, and by the time we had cleaned up from breakfast and Mrs. White had said goodbye, I knew that I had discovered an important truth.

Laci was going to handle this the same way that she saw me handle it.

~ ~ ~

LATER THAT DAY I called all of the kids just as I'd told Laci I'd wanted to. It really had been a good idea and I think each one of them felt better after talking to me in my new and improved mood.

That evening, Laci dropped me off at the restaurant across from the Y that Tanner had suggested and then headed over to pick up Mrs. White (who didn't like to drive after dark anymore). I was waiting in the lobby when Tanner arrived and the hostess led us to our table after we'd pounded one another on the back.

"I saw that the varsity girls only lost one game so far this year," I told Tanner after we'd settled into a booth and ordered our drinks.

"Yeah," he nodded eagerly. "We've got this one chick . . . she's about six-two and she can handle the ball like nothin' you've ever seen. And she's only a *junior*, so as long as she doesn't get injured, next year's lookin' pretty good, too."

"I could be wrong," I said, "but I'm pretty sure 'chick' is a politically incorrect term . . ."

"You sound like Natalie," he said, rolling his eyes at me.

"When do you see Natalie?"

Natalie was one of Laci's best friends and one of Tanner's old girlfriends.

"We get together sometimes," he shrugged.

"And how does her *husband* feel about that?" I smiled.

"I don't know," he smiled right back. "How do *you* feel about it when I get together with Laci?"

(Laci was also one of Tanner's old girlfriends.)

"I hate you, Tanner," I said as the waitress approached the table. "I absolutely hate you."

He grinned at me as she set our drinks down in front of us.

"You wanna talk to me about something," Tanner said after she'd taken our orders and left.

"Yeah," I admitted. "How'd you know?"

"I've known you for over half a century," he laughed.

I smiled back at him.

"So you gonna tell me now or wait until dessert?"

I shrugged at him. "No time like the present, right?"

"Go for it."

I swallowed hard, looked down at my hands, and asked God to help me do something that I hadn't been able to do for forty years.

"You know," I began, "I've had the chance to meet a lot of people who need things over the years."

He nodded.

"And Laci and I've always . . . we've always tried to help them in any way we could, you know, give them food, a place to stay – whatever they've needed."

He nodded again.

"And that's important and everything, but . . ."

"But what?" he asked when I stopped.

I sighed.

"Remember when we went on that mission trip before high school?"

Mike, Laci, Greg, and I had all gone to Mexico with our youth group. Tanner didn't belong to our church and hadn't gone, but he knew what I was talking about.

"Yeah."

"Well," I went on, "Mike and Greg and I met this kid in the landfill. His name was Miguel. He was living in this shack made out of cardboard and his leg was all crippled and–"

"You told me about him," Tanner reminded me.

"Oh. Well, anyway, we really wanted to do something for him, like build him something better to live in or something, but our leader wouldn't let us. He said anything we did would just get torn down and basically we'd be wasting our time. He gave us some things to read to him about Jesus instead and we prayed with him and stuff."

"Uh-huh," Tanner said, clearly having no idea where I was going with this.

"The last day we went there, though," I laughed, "we took all this stuff with us and tried to fix his place up anyway. There wasn't much we could do, but I guess we figured it was better than nothing."

Tanner smiled.

"And Mike was upset afterward. He felt like we hadn't done enough, you know?"

Tanner nodded.

"But Greg said that we did the most important thing, you know – talking to him about Jesus . . . and praying with him? That that was the most important thing. You know what I mean?"

"Sure."

"And so, yeah, sure, Laci and I've done a lot for people over the years by helping them and stuff," I said, "but the most *important* thing we've done is to *pray* with them and tell them about Jesus. Do you understand what I'm saying?"

"Yeah."

"Do you know how many people we've done that for over the years?" I asked him.

"Thousands?"

"Well," I smiled, "maybe not *thousands*, but probably hundreds."

"You and Laci've done a lot of good," he acknowledged.

"But you know how many of those people we actually *know?*" I asked him.

"What do you mean?"

"I mean, most of those people were complete strangers. We never saw them again after we talked to them."

"Okay," he said, looking at me. "What's your point?"

"My point is that we – that *I* – have spent my whole life doing the most important thing for people that I don't even know – people I'll probably never even see again."

"So?"

"So," I said slowly, "what about the people that I *do* know? What about the people that are most important in my life?"

He looked at me carefully and then I saw a flash of realization cross his face.

"*Me?*" he asked in disbelief.

I nodded.

"*That's why we're here?*"

I nodded again.

"So you're all worried that you've spent forty years talking to everybody *else* about God and now you wanna make sure you don't leave me out, is that it?"

"Yeah," I said. "Basically, that's it."

"You've spent *plenty* of time talking to me about God," he informed me dryly.

"No," I disagreed. "I haven't."

He looked at me for a moment and then shook his head back and forth.

"Listen," he said, smiling tightly, "I really appreciate you coming here and everything and I understand what you're trying to do and all, but . . ."

"But what?"

His face turned serious.

"You really shouldn't have wasted your time."

"What do you mean?"

"Look, David," he hesitated. "You're not gonna wanna hear this, but since you brought it up . . ."

"I'm not gonna wanna hear *what?*" I asked, a real knot beginning to form in the pit of my stomach.

He didn't say anything.

76

"*What?*" I finally insisted.

He took a deep breath.

"Do you know what Taoism is?" he finally asked.

"You mean like ying and yang and all that?"

"It's *yin*," he corrected me. "Not ying.

"Taoism," he went on, ignoring my stare, "literally means 'the way of virtue'."

He drew a circle on a napkin and drew an 'S' to separate it into two halves. Then he shaded one side.

"This is yin," he said, pointing to the light side. "It represents the positive forces of good and light and life." Then he pointed to the shaded side. "This is yang. It represents the negative forces of evil and darkness and death. We believe–"

"*We?*" I interrupted him. "Who's *we?*"

"Those of us who follow the Tao," he looked at me and blinked.

I covered my eyes with one hand and propped my elbow on the table.

Oh God, I prayed, *what am I supposed to say to him now?*

"Actually," I heard Tanner saying, "maybe this one's yang and this one's yin. I could never really keep that straight."

I lifted my eyes from my hand and glared at him. He was grinning at me.

"Oh man, Tanner," I said, shaking my head. "See, *this* is why I hate you!"

"That's not a very Christian-like thing to say," he said innocently.

I slumped down in my seat and let out a big, long breath.

"You shoulda seen the look on your face!" he cried, putting his head down on the table. His shoulders were shaking with laughter.

"You know what?" I told him, reaching for my drink. "I couldn't care less if you're saved or not!"

That just made him laugh harder. I took a drink and narrowed my eyes at him, waiting for him to stop laughing.

"I'm sorry," he finally said, sitting up again and wiping his eyes with his hand. He didn't sound one bit sorry. "You're so fun to pick on."

I glared at him some more.

"I'm sorry," he said again, trying to compose himself. "It was very nice of you to try and . . . *witness* to me, but you don't need to worry about it."

I raised an eyebrow at him.

"I'm good," he assured me.

"Define 'good'."

He drummed his fingers on the table, looking mildly uncomfortable.

"What do you want me to say?" he finally asked.

"I wanna know if you're saved or not," I said matter-of-factly.

"I thought you just said you didn't *care* if I was saved or not," he smiled.

"Come on, Tanner . . ."

"Look," he said, "I don't really use words like that and I'm not very good at praying and everything, but . . . don't worry, I believe in God."

"That's not good enough," I said, shaking my head.

"And I read the Bible every day."

"That's not good enough, either."

"That's gonna have to be good enough."

"Tanner," I said, "I'm glad you're reading the Bible and I'm glad you believe in God, but–"

"David," he interrupted me, "why are you all of a sudden so interested in my soul?"

I looked at him for a moment and realized I wasn't going to get any further with him today.

"That's the other reason I'm here," I finally sighed, leaning back in my seat.

"Oh, boy . . . this oughta be good."

I nodded in agreement and he looked at me expectantly.

"Laci and I've actually been in the States for a few days now," I finally began.

"You said you just got in yesterday," he said, looking confused.

"We got in to *Cavendish* yesterday," I explained. "We flew in to Rochester on Sunday. We stayed with Mike. We had some . . . appointments."

"Appointments?"

"Yeah," I nodded.

He didn't say anything.

"At the Mayo Clinic," I clarified, and I watched his face drop. "Don't worry," I added hastily. "They were for *me*, not for Laci."

He continued to stare at me, looking more and more dismayed with each passing second.

"I don't wanna hear this," he finally said quietly.

"No," I admitted. "You don't."

He pressed his lips together, looked away, and shook his head. After a moment he started drumming his fingers on the table again. I gave him some time until he was eventually able to pull himself together long enough to look at me again.

"What?" he demanded at long last. "Go ahead and tell me. What?"

"Early-onset Alzheimer's."

"You?"

I nodded.

"You have early-onset Alzheimer's?"

I nodded again.

"And what exactly does that mean?"

It means that I'm going to forget who you are. It means that I'm going to forget who Laci is. It means I'm going to forget how to feed myself and how to go to the bathroom and I'm going to need constant care and I'm going to ruin Laci's life. It means she's going to spend somewhere between three and fifteen years feeding me and watching me drool.

"You know what Alzheimer's is," I shrugged. "It just means I've got it earlier than usual, that's all."

He was quiet for a minute.

"I'm sorry," he finally managed. "I . . . I really don't know what to say."

"Yeah, I know. Don't worry about it."

"I shouldn't have given you such a hard time when you tried to talk to me. I'm sorry I joked around like that."

"No," I assured him. "It's okay. I want everyone to treat me *normal*, you know?"

He looked at me skeptically.

"I'm serious, Tanner," I said, giving him a half-hearted smile. "If I don't keep my sense of humor about this I'm not going to be able to get through it."

"That implies that you already *have* a sense of humor," he deadpanned and I gave him a real smile.

"That's the spirit!"

"How's Laci handling this?" he asked, immediately serious again.

"I don't know," I sighed, shaking my head. "That's the worst part about it . . . knowing what she's going to have to go through. I can hardly stand to think about it. I don't know how she's going to do it and I feel so sorry for her. She's going to need so much help and I'm not going to be able to do anything for her."

We were quiet for a moment.

"I'll be there for her," he promised quietly.

80

"Ha! I'll bet you will," I laughed. "You've been waiting for years for me to kick the bucket so you could make your move on her."

"David . . ." he looked at me sadly.

"Unfortunately for you," I continued on, ignoring him, "I'm probably going to be around for a long, long time, so you can just keep your big, ugly paws off of Laci."

~ ~ ~

THE NEXT DAY we went to the nursing home to see my dad. We'd been home for two days already and hadn't visited him yet and I felt guilty about that.

I *hated* going to the nursing home to visit my dad.

I felt guilty about that, too.

We found him sitting at the end of the hall, all by himself in his wheelchair, facing a wall.

"Hi, Dad," I said, leaning over, hugging him, and kissing him on his cheek. His face was rough and I wondered when the last time was that someone had given him a shave. Laci leaned down and hugged him too.

"It's me," I told him. "David."

He looked at me and may have nodded, his mouth sagging open slightly. I couldn't tell if he really knew that it was me or not, but he did look me in the eye and I took that as a good sign.

"What are you doing all the way down here?" I asked him. "You wanna go into the lobby or something so Laci and I can sit down and maybe we can visit?"

He possibly nodded again and I got behind his wheelchair and started pushing.

Visit. What a joke.

We settled in to comfortable chairs in a cheery room that wasn't cheery at all, and Laci and I spent thirty minutes "visiting" with him, telling him every detail we could think of about the kids and the grandkids while he sat silently. Then Laci pulled out her phone and showed him some pictures. When she was finished she put her phone away and picked up my dad's hand.

"You wouldn't believe how fast Zoa's growing," she told him, running her thumb over the back of his hand. "I'll have Meredith send some new pictures and next time we come I'll bring those, too, so you can see them, okay?"

We got another possible nod and I saw Laci glance down and look at his hand in her own.

"I'll be right back," she told me, and she got up very suddenly and walked down the hall.

I looked uncomfortably at my dad. Unless I wanted to start talking with him about how I'd spent my week (which I didn't), I was completely out of things to say.

"It's supposed to get really cold by the end of the week," I finally told him. "I was thinking I might put some weather stripping around those windows that are overlooking the deck. I thought I felt some cold air coming in there the other day and that's the side of the house that really seems to get most of the wind so I figured it might be a good idea."

No response. He just stared straight ahead, slack-jawed.

"It looks like Chris took out that bush that was along the sidewalk – you know, that one that was near the light pole? Probably a good idea, I noticed it was looking pretty sad last summer. Maybe we can get down to the nursery in a couple of months and pick out something that'll do better there."

Fortunately Laci wasn't gone too long. She returned, carrying a small, white bottle.

"I got some lotion for your hands," she told my dad, twisting the top of it off and shaking some of it out. She sat back down in front of him and picked up his hand again. She looked up at me. "They're really rough."

I nodded at her and watched as she slowly rubbed the lotion into the skin on his fingers and onto the back of his hand. I don't know how she did it, but she managed to find more stuff to talk to him about as she did. After a moment he closed his eyes and something that might have passed for a smile crossed his lips.

"Does that feel good, Dad?" I asked. He nodded. There was no question about it this time. He nodded.

Laci glanced at me and I smiled at her. She smiled back.

I settled back into my chair and watched her as she talked effortlessly to my dad, gently massaging lotion into his hands.

That evening Laci and I went to the high school to watch a basketball game and afterward we went out to eat with Tanner.

"What time are Jordan and Charlotte coming tomorrow?" he asked after he'd been through the buffet line for a third time.

"They'll be here in time for lunch," I explained.

"Oh."

"You wanna come?"

"I can't," he said. "I'm teaching a class, remember?"

Tanner was a certified conceal-and-carry instructor – I did remember that – but I didn't remember that he was teaching a class tomorrow. I wasn't sure if that was an "Alzheimer's forget" or a "normal forget," so I just nodded.

"Have you talked to them?" I asked.

"I talked to Jordan last night," he admitted.

"And?" I prodded when he didn't say anything else.

Tanner shrugged and shook his head. I sighed.

"She's going to be fine," Laci said, taking my hand.

I glanced away.

"She will be," Tanner agreed. "You know how she is."

I looked at Tanner and felt sad, thinking about everything Charlotte had already been through . . . and about everything that lay ahead of her. Mrs. White was doing great *now*, but people can only live for so long. And she had Jordan to worry about and now the fact that she was going to lose me . . .

I glanced at Laci. She looked sad too, and I suddenly remembered that I was supposed to be keeping a positive attitude.

"You're right," I told Tanner, nodding. "All Charlotte needs is to take it out on someone for a little while and then she'll get over it and be fine.

"Poor Jordan," I went on sadly, sighing and shaking my head. I smiled at Laci and she laughed.

"It might be *you* that she takes it out on!" Tanner said. "She might be saving it all up for tomorrow."

"I'm slowly dying from dementia!" I protested. "She's not going to take it out on me!"

"Maybe not," Tanner agreed, "but I'd be ready for anything if I were you."

"I know," I smiled. "I am."

I glanced at Laci and she gave me another smile. Silently I marveled again at my newfound power to influence her mood.

"Hey," Tanner said. "You wanna play racquetball in the morning? My class doesn't start until ten . . ."

I glanced at Laci, who gave me a "go ahead" shrug.

"Sure," I agreed. "Pick me up at seven."

Apparently the fact that I was "slowly dying from dementia" didn't make Tanner feel as if he needed to take it easy on me on the racquetball court or anything.

"I see this new medicine you're on has done wonders for your backhand," he noted sardonically the next morning after he soundly beat me in our first three games.

I smirked at him.

"Wanna go for the best outta seven?" he suggested with a malicious smile.

"What do you mean?" I asked seriously.

"Wanna go again?"

"Huh?"

"Do you wanna play another game?"

"What do you mean?" I asked again.

"What do you mean, *'What do I mean'*?"

"Do I know you?" I asked slowly.

He took his goggles off and looked at me, a distraught expression on his face. I looked at him blankly for another moment and then finally gave him a malicious smile of my own.

"See?" I said, bouncing the ball off his forehead and heading up to the serving box. "I'm not the only one who's fun to pick on!"

~ ~ ~

A FEW HOURS later, Jordan and Charlotte's car pulled into the driveway. When I heard a door slam shut, I went to the window and saw Jordan striding up the walkway.

I watched carefully, looking for any hints in Jordan's movement that might indicate symptoms of Huntington's, the disease that had claimed the life of his and Tanner's brother, Chase, years earlier. Huntington's disease is inherited, and once Chase had been diagnosed it had meant that there was a fifty-fifty chance that either Tanner or Jordan would have it as well. Tanner had immediately gotten himself tested and found out that he did *not* have Huntington's, but Jordan–

The doorbell rang and I opened the door.

"Hi!" I said, giving him a hug.

"How you doing, Dave?" he asked, pounding me on the back.

"Not bad," I said. "Not bad. How 'bout you?"

"Not bad," he smiled.

"Where's Charlotte?"

"She'll be right in," he answered.

But a few minutes passed and Charlotte still didn't arrive. Laci came into the living room and greeted Jordan and we stood by the door and talked, and finally I peeked through the blinds into the driveway and saw that Charlotte was still sitting in the passenger seat, staring out her window, looking away from the house.

"She's having a hard time," Jordan said quietly from behind me, laying a hand on my shoulder. "I'll go get her."

"No," I told him, shaking my head. "I'll go."

I walked out the front door and down the sidewalk to the driveway. Charlotte glanced toward the house, saw me coming, and quickly turned her head away from me. I heard her lock the doors.

I tried the handle of the driver's side anyway.

"Charlotte," I said loudly, tapping on the window. "Let me in."

She shook her head, still not looking at me. All of a sudden the doors unlocked, but Charlotte hadn't moved. I glanced back at the living room window and saw Jordan pointing a remote at the car. Surprised, Charlotte looked up at him too and then – realizing what he'd done – recovered in time to relock the doors before I could get in. Together they unlocked and locked the doors another time or two before I managed to try the handle at just the right moment and open the door, but as I climbed in, Charlotte immediately reached for her door handle and tried to get out. I grabbed the sleeve of her jacket and stopped her.

"How old are you?" I asked. "Ten?"

At that, she let go of the door handle and covered her face with her hands, sobbing.

I let go of her jacket and wrapped my arms around her. She let me pull her close and then buried her head against my chest, weeping. I just held her for a while as she sobbed.

"It's okay," I said softly after she'd quieted down a bit.

"I don't want this to be happening," she whispered, still against my chest.

"I know," I said, squeezing her, "but it's going to be okay."

She pulled away from me slightly and looked at me.

"How?" she demanded. "How is it going to be okay?"

I didn't answer her, but I took her hand and held it tight. We looked at each other for a long moment.

"I love you," she finally said, breaking down and crying against my shoulder again.

"I know," I said, squeezing her hand. "I love you, too."

Finally she managed to pull herself together and she sat back with a look of resolve on her face.

"Neurological diseases *suck!*" she said, wiping her sleeve across her face. I gave her a little smile.

"How's Jordan doing, anyway?" I asked. "He looks good."

"He is," Charlotte agreed. "No symptoms."

I gave her a bigger smile.

"Can we go in now?" I asked her. "Or do you want to sit out here in the car and pout some more?"

She looked at me for moment.

"I want to pout," she finally decided.

"It's too cold out here. Come on." I gave her one more smile, and then I promised, "You can pout inside."

~ ~ ~

MONDAY I CALLED my boss, Josef, and told him what was going on.

I also quit my job.

Okay, technically, I didn't quit . . . I retired. And, technically, I didn't even retire, because Josef insisted that they wanted to contract me as a "special consultant" on the addition to the orphanage. Both of us knew this was nothing more than a pity gesture, but it was one that I gratefully accepted.

"How did it go?" Laci asked when I got off the phone.

"Fine," I said. I told her that I was still going to get to work with Dorito on the addition and she smiled at me in an understanding way – this was the first project that Dorito and I'd had the chance to work on together.

Now it would also be the last.

"You'll have to call Dorito and tell him," she said, and I nodded. Then she hit me with a bombshell by adding, "I quit too."

Laci and I had talked for several days about whether or not I should quit. I knew that my company would have worked with me – allowed me to stay on in whatever capacity I felt capable of, but I also knew that from that point on, someone would always be double-checking everything that I did, and I wasn't really interested in having someone question every move that I made.

We had never talked – even for the briefest moment – about *her* quitting.

"You what?"

"I quit," she repeated.

"You quit," I said flatly.

She nodded.

"Why in the *world* would you quit?"

"Because," she said, shrugging again, "you're not going to be working anymore and I want to spend time with you."

"You're just going to sit around and visit with me all day?" An image flashed through my mind of Laci massaging my hands with lotion.

"Well, no," she said, "I thought we would go *do* stuff . . . you know – travel and stuff?"

"Travel?"

"Yeah. Go do all the things we've always wanted to do."

"Like what?"

"Well," she said, "we could go to the Keys and Seattle and Carlsbad Caverns and–"

"Carlsbad Caverns?!" I laughed. "Since when have you wanted to go to Carlsbad Caverns?"

"I . . . I've always wanted to go there."

"No, you haven't," I argued. "*I've* always wanted to go to Carlsbad Caverns. *You've* always wanted to help little orphans down in Mexico – and that's what I want, too. I want to go back there and both of us can help out."

"No," she said, shaking her head adamantly. "We're not going back."

"Laci!" I cried. "What are you talking about? It's bad enough that *I* had to quit *my* job! I'm not gonna let *you* quit too!"

"I already did," she reminded me. (Not that this mattered at all – both of us knew that they'd take her back in a heartbeat.) "I don't *want* to go back to work – I want to spend time with you!"

"What are you gonna do? Sit around all day and watch me twiddle my thumbs?"

"No – we're going to go *do* things," she reminded me.

"I . . . I really appreciate what you're trying to do here," I assured her, taking her hand, "but realistically, honey, there's probably going to be a limit to how much we're going to be able to *do*."

"Why?" she asked, "you're doing great!"

"Sure, right now I am," I agreed, "but I'm not going to be this way forever – who knows how long it's going to last?" (According to everything I'd been able to read online about my medicine, I had between nine months and three years before things started going downhill again.)

"Well, we're going to take advantage of it right now and do stuff while we can." She looked at me stubbornly. "We're not going back to Mexico."

"And then what? Once I get so I can't travel or whatever, *then* are you going to sit around and watch me twiddle my thumbs?" Actually it was probably going to be more like sitting around and watching me drool on myself, but I didn't say that. "Laci . . . I want you to be able keep working . . . I want you to keep doing what you love!"

"Do you honestly think I'm going to love going off to work every day while I'm worried about you?"

"That's why you need to put me somewhere," I muttered.

"Where?" she asked calmly. "Some nice nursing home in Mexico City so you can have a bunch of *'quack doctors who got their medical degrees off the back of a cereal box'* talking to you all day in Spanish?"

I sighed, shook my head, and looked away. And then I started thinking about what she was suggesting.

We *would* be closer to better health care once those little blue wonder pills stopped working their magic . . . and closer to clinical trials too if we decided to try one of those. Not only that, but we'd also be closer to most of the kids – it would be easier for them to come and visit us . . . easier for them to come and help Laci.

I thought about what it would be like for Laci once I wasn't able to do anything anymore. And I thought about what – if anything – would make Laci the happiest once that time came. And I knew that what Laci wanted – no . . . what she *needed* – was to be able to do everything in her power to make me happy and to take care of me the very best way that she could.

And I realized in an instant that this was what I needed to let her do.

I looked at her – at this *gift* that she wanted so desperately to give to me – and I saw that if I would take it, I would be giving her a gift right back.

I put my arms around her and looked into her eyes and I thought how glad I was that God had given this woman to me to be my wife.

"Okay," I finally nodded.

Immediately I knew I had made the right decision because she gave me the broadest smile I'd seen from her in months.

"But can we go to Portland, too?" I asked as she smiled at me happily.

"Oregon?" she wanted to know, "Or Maine?"

"Both," I answered.

~ ~ ~

BEFORE WE MADE any arrangements to start traveling to Portland or the Keys or anywhere else, we decided that we'd better take care of some of the most important projects around the house in order to make it livable. Dorito put our home in Mexico on the market for us, and we made arrangements with Jessica that Laci and I would buy Dad's as soon as ours in Mexico sold. I think Jess was glad we weren't going back to Mexico (and especially glad that Dad's house was going to be *our* problem now).

We spent a day at the giant mega-hardware store picking out what we wanted and then I started working on the kitchen counters while Laci began painting and wallpapering the master bedroom.

I'd always enjoyed do-it-yourself projects in the past, but we'd both been at it hard and heavy for about three days when I unplugged the tile saw and went into the bedroom. Laci was balanced on a ladder, edging the ceiling.

"Laci?"

"What?" she asked, not taking her eyes from her edger.

I walked over to the ladder and peered up at her.

"This isn't what I want to be doing," I told her.

She looked down at me.

"Huh?"

"I don't want to fix up the house," I said. "This isn't how I want to be spending my time."

She looked down and stared at me meaningfully for a moment.

"I thought this was what you wanted to do," she finally said.

"I know," I admitted, "I thought it was too, but it's not. This isn't what I want to be doing."

She looked down at me for another moment and then set her edger in the roller tray and descended the ladder, one step at a time. When she was standing next to me she asked, "What *do* you want to be doing?"

"I have some ideas," I said, grinning and raising my eyebrows at her.

"I have to finish this wall while the edge is still wet," she said, pointing at the ceiling and trying not to smile.

"And then?"

"And then we'll see."

"Boy," I said disappointedly. "I thought we were doing things that I wanted to do!"

"I really can't quit until this wall's done," she said earnestly.

"Fine," I said, hanging my head. "I'll go back to the kitchen. Hopefully I won't cut any fingers off."

"I won't be long," she promised.

"Uh-huh," I said dejectedly, and I went back to my tile saw.

It actually didn't take very long for her to finish the wall and we spent the rest of the afternoon together in the master bedroom amidst the smell of fresh paint and wallpaper paste.

"This is much better than fixing the house up," I told Laci as we lay next to each other.

She smiled at me.

"We have to finish, though," she said. "We can't live here like this . . . this place is a disaster!"

Coming from Laci (who could overlook just about anything), this was a true testament of how bad things actually were.

"We can hire someone to come in and do it," I promised. "It's just that this is not how I want to be spending my time."

"And this is?" she smiled at me.

I grinned back, but then I stopped and searched her eyes for a moment.

"Are you disappointed?"

"Disappointed?" she asked, propping herself up on one elbow. "Are you kidding? I hate decorating and stuff!"

"You do?"

She nodded at me emphatically.

"Then why did you agree that we should fix up the house!?" I cried.

"Because I thought that's what you wanted to do," she answered meekly.

"Laci!"

"What?"

I just shook my head, exasperated. How had I not realized before now that I needed to figure out what *Laci* wanted to do and then make it seem as if it was *my* idea?

"I think we should visit the kids," I finally said. "One at a time. We'll start with the youngest and work our way up."

"You want to go to Australia?" she asked, excitement growing in her voice.

"Ay, Mate!" I said in my very best Australian accent. "Let's ring up Marco and tell 'im we're flying across the big pond!"

"Don't talk like that," Laci said with a mortified look on her face. "You have a terrible Australian accent!"

"Blimey," I replied.

~ ~ ~

BY THE END of the first week in February we'd mapped out most of our plans to visit the kids. In the end, we decided to wait to go to Australia until Easter since Marco wasn't going to have much time off until then. Three of the girls lived close enough that we could go visit just for a day or two anytime we wanted, and we bought tickets to fly to California to see Grace at the very end of the month.

Dorito's wife, Maria, came from a small town only about an hour east of Cavendish and her family still lived there, so Dorito and his family came home often enough that it wasn't really necessary to plan a trip to Mexico. I still wanted to go down there, however, so that Laci could visit the orphanage, but before I could make any definite plans (I was leaning toward summer . . . after Grace's wedding in June), Dorito called with plans of his own.

"Hi, Dad!" he said as soon as I answered my phone.

"Hey, Dorito," I said. "What's up?"

"Remember how we've always talked about going salmon fishing with Tanner in Alaska?"

"Uhhh, I remember that you and *Tanner* have always talked about going salmon fishing in Alaska and that occasionally you mention bringing me along when you realize that I'm standing there listening and feeling left out."

"Dad . . ." he said, sounding wounded.

"Truth hurts, doesn't it?"

"Dad . . ." he said again.

I decided to let him off the hook.

"Are you seriously thinking about going?" I asked.

"Yeah," he said, the excitement returning to his voice. "Ten days – this July. We can catch the end of the king season, the beginning of the sockeye season, and that's right when the halibut are coming into the bays to spawn."

"You've already talked to Tanner about this and planned it all out, haven't you?"

"Well," he said hesitantly, "I talked to him."

I paused for a minute.

"I . . . I don't know, Dorito," I finally said. "I don't really want to leave your mom for that long."

"Mom could come down here!" he insisted. "She could spend some time with Maria and the kids and visit the orphanage–"

"You've already planned it all out with her too, haven't you?"

"I might have mentioned it," he admitted.

I closed my eyes and sighed quietly. *It had started already . . . the talking behind my back . . . conspiring with one another . . . planning my entire life out for me.*

"I don't suppose Marco can come?" I asked.

"No," he answered.

"Okay," I said. "So it's you, me, and Tanner?"

"Yeah," he responded. "Ya wanna do it?"

"Absolutely," I said. "Let's go."

A few days before Valentine's Day I announced to Laci that I wanted to go shopping.

"Okay," she said, nodding and getting up from the couch.

"No," I clarified. "I want to go by myself."

She stopped and looked at me, alarmed.

"I'll be fine," I told her. "I promise."

"But I . . . I thought you weren't going to drive anymore," Laci said, looking dismayed.

98

"Well, I wasn't," I admitted, "but this medicine's working so good that I think I'll be fine. I'm pretty much back to my old self."

I'd been on the Coceptiva for about three weeks now and I just knew that I hadn't been having any more problems.

"Why can't I go with you?" she asked.

"Because I'm going to buy you your Valentine's present and I don't want you to see it."

"I won't look," she promised. "I'll take you wherever you want to go and you can go in all by yourself and I'll just wait in the car."

It actually wouldn't have really mattered if she'd gone with me, but I was getting really sick of being constantly chaperoned everywhere I went. Plus, I couldn't remember the last time I'd had a few unsupervised minutes to myself.

"No," I said, shaking my head. "I don't even want you to know where I get it from."

"Then you can have Tanner take you," she suggested, "or Jessica."

"I'll be fine. I want to go by myself."

She looked at me

"I . . . I don't think you should be driving," she said, shaking her head slightly. I took a few steps toward her and put my hands on her arms.

"This medicine's *working*," I told her again. "I can feel it. I'm back to my old self again. I'll be fine."

"David," she began, but then she stopped. She looked as if she might cry at any moment.

"What?"

She held my gaze.

"You aren't back to your old self," she said quietly.

I looked at her, trying to register what she was saying.

"What?" I finally asked, trying unsuccessfully to keep the alarm out of my voice.

"You aren't back to your old self," she said again, gently.

I looked back at her for a moment and then dropped my hands from her arms. I stepped away from her and walked to the couch, sitting down. She followed and sat next to me, putting one of her hands on mine.

I didn't say anything for a minute. I just closed my eyes and rubbed my forehead with my free hand, trying to make sense of it all.

I had been sure . . . so *sure* that those little blue pills had been working. But now? To find out that they really hadn't been?

I was at a complete loss for words.

"What have I been doing?" I finally asked, looking at her. I didn't really want to hear the answer, but I knew that I needed to know.

"You haven't really been doing anything," Laci admitted.

"I've been forgetting things?" I guessed.

"Well, no," she hedged, "not really."

"What then?"

"You just . . . you just haven't been yourself."

"What do you mean?"

"I don't know," she said, giving me an evasive shrug. "You're just acting different."

"What am I doing that's any different from what I usually do?"

"You're just . . . your personality is *different*," she finally said reluctantly. "I don't really know how to explain it."

"My personality is different." I repeated slowly.

"Yes," she nodded. "And I've been reading about how one of the symptoms can be a change in personality."

"My personality isn't any different!" I cried.

"Yes it is!" she argued. "I don't know if it's the Alzheimer's or if it's one of the side effects from that medicine or whatever, but you're definitely acting different."

"Like how?"

"Like . . ." She hesitated before telling me. "Like you're not as upset about things as you normally would be."

100

"Upset about what things?"

"About everything that's been happening," she said. "About being diagnosed and everything."

I looked at her. "Huh?"

"Normally," she explained patiently, "if you were to find out that you had Alzheimer's disease, you'd be *upset*. You'd be acting more . . . more unhappy . . . more depressed."

"I *was* upset!" I cried.

"Yeah," she admitted, "at first. But now you're not."

"So because I'm *handling* things well I can't drive?!" I exclaimed.

"I'm just saying that obviously something weird is going on," she said. "You're not yourself!"

I looked at her in disbelief, hardly able to believe what I was hearing. It was all I could do to keep from laughing out loud at her.

"Would you like for me to be grumpy?" I asked her seriously. "I can get grumpy real fast."

She looked at me quizzically.

"Laci," I said, smiling at her and pulling her toward me. "Come here."

I sat back on the couch and put my arm around her, kissing her on the forehead.

"This is me," I told her. "This is totally me."

She looked at me uncertainly.

"Really," I promised. "Look. I'm sorry if I have been *so* unpleasant to live with for the past thirty-three years that—"

"I never said you were unpleasant to live with!" she interrupted.

"Just unhappy and depressed?"

"I never said that!"

"Yes, you did," I argued. "You said that I was unhappy and depressed."

"Well . . . just when something's wrong."

"And how am I the rest of the time?" I asked. "Jovial?"

She couldn't help but smile.

"So anyway," I went on, giving her a smile back, "I'm sorry that I've been such a terrible person to live with for the past thirty-three years, but just because I'm not unhappy and depressed doesn't mean that I'm symptomatic."

I could tell that she still wasn't convinced.

"Look, Laci," I said, shifting on the couch so that I could look at her directly. "I made a decision . . . a *conscious* decision that I was going to accept this and have a positive attitude about it."

"Really?" she asked quietly.

I nodded and she looked at me suspiciously.

"But that's not really like you," she noted.

"No," I admitted. "You're right. It's not."

"So why the change?"

Laci looked at me expectantly, but I was hesitant to go on. I couldn't tell her that the reason for my attitude change was a sudden revelation that things were going to be a lot easier on her if she didn't have to put up with my griping and complaining. If I did, she wasn't going to believe that the change she'd seen in me was genuine . . . that it was real.

But it was.

My cheerful demeanor may have started out as a simple attempt to make things easier for Laci, but it hadn't taken long for my attitude to actually change. I'd heard the old saying for my entire life – *Happiness is a choice* – but I had never believed it before now (or at least I had never tried it). Now I knew that it was true, however. No matter what's going on in your life, you can *choose* to be happy.

But how was I going to explain this to Laci?

"Every time God does something in my life that's not what I want," I began carefully, "I always fight Him on it . . . right?"

She nodded.

"But eventually I figure out that He knew what He was doing and I can see how He was in control and everything and then finally, I come around, you know?"

102

She nodded again.

"But it usually takes me a really long time to get to that point," I said. "Right?"

"Right."

I looked at her for a moment.

"Well," I finally said quietly, "I don't have a really long time anymore."

She looked back at me and didn't say anything. Her eyes started shining with tears.

I pulled her closer and went on.

"I just want to go ahead and jump right to that place where I realize how much God loves me and where I know that everything that's happening is going to work for good. Do you know what I mean?"

She gave me a tiny nod.

"I want to be *happy*," I said, squeezing her. "I want for *us* to be happy."

She gave me a small smile.

"What do you say, Laci?" I asked, smiling back. "Do you want to be happy with me?"

She gave me a bigger nod and a bigger smile and then she wrapped her arms around me and buried her face against me.

And after that, I got to drive.

~ ~ ~

ON VALENTINE'S DAY I made pancakes for Laci (which was rather disastrous, but I think she appreciated it nonetheless) and I served them to her in bed. She bravely attempted to eat several bites and then I promised her she could have some cereal after she opened her presents.

"I got you something too," she said, anxiously leaning over to set the tray on the floor and resurfacing with a package.

I took it from her and unwrapped it. It was a journal with a picture of an elephant on the front and a pen attached with a leather tab.

"What's this?" I asked.

"Remember that old movie we saw . . . *The Notebook*?"

"No."

"With James Garner?"

"No."

"Where his wife had Alzheimer's?"

"Was it a chick flick?" I asked her.

"Not really."

"Because if it was a chick flick, I can pretty much guarantee you I won't remember it."

"Maybe it was," she admitted.

"So what about it?"

"Okay," she said with growing excitement. "Well, it's this really great movie . . . as a matter of fact, we should watch it again–"

"I only have three to twenty years left, Laci. I'm not going to spend any of it watching a chick flick."

"You could read the book . . ."

"Do you wanna get to the point here?" I asked her, whirling my finger in a "speed it up" fashion. "My brain's not getting any younger."

"Okay, well, anyway, she has Alzheimer's, but before she gets bad she writes down all this stuff she doesn't want to forget and then," Laci said, "after she gets bad her husband reads it to her all the time to remind her of all the things she wanted to remember."

"What kind of stuff?"

"Well," Laci said. "She wrote down all about her husband and how they fell in love and everything."

She looked at me expectantly.

"So I thought maybe you'd wanna do that," she went on, tapping the cover. "See? It has an elephant on the front. You know – 'an elephant never forgets'?"

"You want me to write down how we fell in love?" I asked her skeptically.

"No, it doesn't have to be that," she said hastily, "it can be anything. You can write down whatever you want – anything that you don't want to forget."

"Uh-huh," I said slowly.

She looked disappointed.

"But, I mean, don't feel like you *have* to use it or anything," she went on. "It was just a thought. It's okay if you don't like it."

"No, no," I said. "I think it's a great idea."

"Really?" she asked, brightening up.

"Oh, yeah. As a matter of fact, I think I'm gonna write something in it right now."

"Really?" she said again. She looked quite happy now.

"Uh-huh," I nodded, pulling the pen out. I tilted the journal so she couldn't see what I was doing.

"There," I said, closing it when I was done.

"Can I see what you wrote?" she asked.

"No!" I said. "It's private!"

"But . . . if I'm going to read it to you one day, I'm gonna have to see it anyway."

"Well, okay," I finally conceded. "I guess you can hear it now."

She nestled closer to me and I started reading what I'd written.

Dear Dave–

The first thing you need to know is that you have a beautiful wife. Her name is Laci.

Laci looked at me and smiled. I smiled back. Then I kept reading.

Ever since you were a little boy, she has been trying to drive you crazy. Well guess what? She's finally succeeded!

Laci swatted at me and I laughed.

"You want yours now?" I asked, reaching into the nightstand on my side of the bed and pulling out an envelope.

"No," she said, crossing her arms at me. "You're not my Valentine anymore."

"I-bet-you-know-what's-in-here . . ." I sang, tipping the envelope back and forth.

Laci – who neither wanted nor needed *anything* – was a particularly difficult person to buy presents for. Once I'd finally struck upon something that she really liked (buying items through a Christian organization – in her name – to give to impoverished third-world families), I'd stuck with it. Last year I'd bought a cow or something and she'd really seemed to like that, so I'd gone with livestock again this year.

"Fine," she said, not able to resist finding out what I'd bought and snatching the envelope out of my hand. She ripped the envelope open and pulled out a sheet of paper.

"Oh!" she said happily. "A sheep!"

"Not just one sheep," I informed her. "*Six* sheep. That's practically a whole flock. A whole flock of sheep that are walking around with the name 'Laci' shaved into their sides."

She laughed and gave me a long kiss.

"Thank you," she said. "What else did you get me?"

"What else?"

"You went to the *store* the other day," she reminded me. "To get me a Valentine's present. You didn't get this from the store."

"Really?"

She nodded.

"Oh," I said, reaching over to the nightstand again. "I guess that must be what this is."

I could tell she wasn't sure if I was playing with her or not.

"What is it?" she asked as she took the package from me.

"I don't know," I shrugged. "Open it and find out."

She opened it and glanced at me uncertainly, obviously worried that letting me drive the other day had *not* been a good idea.

"What is it?" I asked her innocently.

"It's . . . it's Play-doh."

"Play-doh?"

"Uh-huh."

"Do you like it?" I asked her.

"Sure . . ." she said, slowly nodding.

"Why did I get you Play-doh?" I asked, trying not to smile.

"Because," she answered carefully. "Everybody likes Play-doh."

"Everybody likes Play-doh?" I burst out laughing and she looked at me, relieved.

"So," she smiled, "you're aware that this is perhaps *not* the most romantic gift you've ever gotten me?"

"Yes," I smiled. "I'm *completely* aware, but it's nice to see how sweet you're planning on being to me when I'm not."

She smiled back at me.

"But you're wrong about one thing," I told her. "This happens to be a *very* romantic gift."

"It is?"

"Uh-huh."

"And how do you figure that?"

"Because," I said, brushing her hair out of her face and tucking it behind her ear. "When we were in preschool together we used to hide under the stairs together and taste Play-doh."

"We did?"

"Uh-huh. You don't remember doing that?"

"No," she said. "I mean, I believe you, but I don't remember it."

"Well, I do."

"But why did you buy this for me?" she asked, still confused.

"Because no matter what happens," I told her, "I'm never going to forget that."

She looked at me and smiled.

"And I wanted to let you know," I went on, "that I'm never going to forget you either."

Dorito called later that day with more big plans. In addition to the fishing trip we were planning for the summer, he thought that all three of us should all go elk hunting in Montana in the fall. (This was another big idea that he and Tanner had often talked about over the years, only occasionally remembering to include me in their plans as an afterthought.)

Since this was another opportunity for Laci to go to Mexico and visit the orphanage (and since I really wanted to go elk hunting in Montana), I readily agreed.

"I'll take care of everything!" he promised once I'd told him that I'd love to go.

"Don't forget though," I advised, "Tanner's gonna want to do something where we hike in or ride four-wheelers . . . nothing with horses."

"I *know* Dad," Dorito said, sounding quite annoyed that I felt it necessary to remind him of something so obvious. "Don't worry – I've got it handled."

That night, we went out to dinner. We had just started eating our salads when I heard someone say my name.

"David?"

I looked up.

It was my old high school girlfriend, Samantha.

"Sam!" I said, standing up and giving her a hug. "How are you doing?"

"I'm good," she replied, then she looked at Laci and smiled. "Hi, Laci."

"Hey, Sam," Laci smiled back.

"Are you still living near Memphis?" I asked her.

"Yeah," she nodded. "Mom just had a heart catheterization done so I flew up to spend the week with her."

"Everything go okay?"

"Yeah, pretty good."

"Lovely way to spend Valentine's Day," I said.

"Tell me about it."

"How's your dad?" I asked.

"He's good," she said, nodding toward an older gentleman who was seated alone at a table across the room. "We just came out to grab some dinner. How's your dad doing?"

"Well," I said, tipping my hand back and forth. "So-so . . . you know how it goes."

"Yeah. It's hard to watch them get old, isn't it?"

I nodded.

"You and Mark still both with the same company?"

She and her husband Mark were both computer engineers.

"Nu-unh," she shook her head. "Mark and I got divorced last year."

"Oh! I'm sorry to hear that." I said. I really was.

"Yeah . . . as soon as Zack went off to college . . ." she said, shaking her head. "I guess he was ready for something else."

"I'm sorry," I said again.

"Thanks," she smiled. "It's all right though. At least I found out while I'm young. I've still got my whole life ahead of me, right?"

"Absolutely," I nodded.

"So how have you two been?" she asked, looking at Laci.

"Great," Laci answered.

Sam looked back to me. "Everybody healthy and happy?"

"Yeah," I nodded. "We've got nothing to complain about."

"She looks fantastic," Laci said after Sam had gone back to her table.

"Does she?" I said. "I didn't notice."

"Liar."

"What can I say, Laci? I've always had great taste in women."

"Well," Laci said. "Apparently she's free . . . here's your big chance!"

"Really?!" I asked, starting to get out of my chair. "You don't mind? Thanks!"

"You go right ahead!"

"You think I won't do it!"

She laughed.

"Ahhh," I said, sitting back down. "I guess I'll just stick with what I've got."

"Gee, thanks," she smirked.

"I am sorry to hear about them getting divorced, though," I said seriously. "That's too bad."

"She seems to have a pretty good attitude about it," Laci said.

"Well," I smiled, "you know what they say. Attitude is everything."

That night, lying in bed with Laci, I found myself thinking about my conversation with Sam.

"Laci?" I said in the darkness.

"What?"

"I want you to know something."

"What?" She was lying like she always did, with her head nestled on my shoulder and her arm across my chest.

"I want you to know that I've always been faithful to you. I don't want you to ever wonder about that one day."

She actually started *laughing*.

"What's so funny?" I asked her.

"I'm sorry," she said, reaching up to wipe her eye. "That was very sweet."

"Then why are you laughing?"

"Well," she said. "I've just never really worried about it, that's all."

"Never?"

"No."

"Well, you should, Laci! You should worry about that a lot!"

She laughed again.

"Is it THAT funny?" I asked her. "Are you *so sure* I never had an affair?"

"Yeah," she nodded. "I'm pretty sure."

"Why?" I asked her. "You think no one else would want me?"

"No," she said, patting her hand against my chest. "I'm sure many, *many* women have wanted you over the years."

"That's right!" I told her. "You have no idea how many women I've had to fight off since I've been married to you."

"Uh-huh," she said, hugging me.

"I really could've had an affair, you know," I said, hugging her back.

"With who?"

"I don't know," I shrugged. "Inez maybe? I could've found somebody."

She laughed one more time.

"Don't you want to know if I've been faithful?" she asked after we'd laid there quietly for a minute.

"Nope," I said. "I know you have been."

"How do you know?"

"Because I trust you," I said, running my finger down the side of her face. "I trust you with my life."

~ ~ ~

DURING THE NEXT two weeks we visited each of the girls who lived nearby, and at the end of February we flew to California to see Grace. I was bored out of my skull while Grace and Laci talked about plans for the wedding, but Laci seemed really excited about it so I pretended to care whether or not the dinner menu included a vegan option or if the color of the ribbons in the bridesmaid's hair complemented the groomsmen's boutonnieres.

After spending a week with Grace, we flew directly from California to Florida to spend a few – a *very* few – days with Laci's dad.

Our relationship with Laci's dad had gone downhill after Laci's mom had died, due in no small part to his new wife. Within three months of the death of Laci's mom, he had remarried and moved to Florida. Even Laci (who always tried very hard to find the good in every person she'd ever met) had a hard time finding *anything* good about her new stepmom, Peggy.

Peggy was, quite frankly, a narcissistic gossip who, whenever we visited, worried constantly that having "strangers" in the house was upsetting to her Yorkshire terrier (an annoying little animal that – on more than one occasion – I'd had the desire to dropkick). We usually got ourselves a hotel room, but just being around her for the shortest periods of time managed to leave me with the strongest desire to lie down in a dark, quiet room with a cool cloth on my eyes.

Fortunately, however, Peggy was also a hypochondriac, which meant that she frequently "wasn't feeling well enough" to accompany Laci's dad whenever he took us out to eat, offered to take us to the beach, or invited us to go golfing.

When we arrived on this particular visit, Peggy was in a rampage because she claimed that a neighbor had installed blinds that were "against code" (in other words, she didn't like the color). She spent most of our first day there on the phone with members of the Homeowners Association, dissecting the definition of "window treatment" with anyone who would listen. Finally the president of the Homeowners Association determined that "window treatment" only referred to drapes and curtains and that the offending blinds could stay. Peggy got herself in such a huff about this that for the next two days (when she wasn't threatening to move), she sequestered herself and her stupid little dog in the bedroom, saying that the incident had been too upsetting for her to visit.

Darn.

Personally, I made a point of going for a walk when I noticed that the renegade neighbor was out front, pulling weeds from around her mailbox.

"Hello," I said brightly as I walked by.

"Hi," she smiled, looking up at me.

"Beautiful day," I said.

"Yes, it is," she agreed.

"Hey! Are those new blinds?" I asked, motioning to her house.

"Yes," she said. "We just got them last week."

"Oh," I nodded. "I really like them. That's a great color."

~ ~ ~

DORITO CALLED THE week after we got home from Florida.

"I can't go to Montana with you," were the first words out of his mouth.

"What?!" I exclaimed. "Why not?!"

"Maria's pregnant."

"*Again?*" (This would be their fifth.)

"Yes," he answered. "Again."

"I don't understand how this happened," I said, exasperated.

"Well, you see, Dad," Dorito began, "when a man and a woman love each other very much . . ."

"Very funny. What I *meant* was that I can't believe she's having another baby. She just had Erin like five months ago!"

"It was *eight* months ago, Dad."

I sighed.

"So you can't go hunting now just because she's pregnant?"

"She's due the same day we're supposed to fly out!" Dorito exclaimed. "I can't be gone then!"

"Well, what if we can change our reservations?"

"To when?" Dorito asked. "Even if we got a spot at the beginning of the season, what if she goes early again like she did with Catie?"

"What if we got a spot at the *end* of the season?" I suggested.

"I'm not going to go away for ten days and leave her here with four kids and a brand-new baby!"

I sighed again.

"Why don't we just cancel it and go next year?" I asked.

"No," Dorito said emphatically. "You and Tanner just need to go without me."

It hung, unspoken in the air, that there was a good chance I wouldn't be in any shape to go anywhere the following fall.

"Are you still going with us to Alaska?"

"Yeah," he said. "I think so. As long as everything goes good."

"Well, do you think you and Maria could at least manage to give me a grand*son* this time?"

"No promises," Dorito said, "but the sonogram's in two months. I'll let you know what we find out."

My fifty-fifth birthday was two weeks later and we had a great celebration. Everyone except for Marco was able to come, and after that we flew to Australia and spent ten days with him, practicing our Australian accents and sampling Vegemite sandwiches and shrimp on the barbie.

We never did make it to either one of the Portlands or to Carlsbad Caverns, but we did fly to Florida again in late May to see Laci's dad (and Peggy) and after one day of visiting (quite enough, thank you) we rented a car and drove to the Keys for a few days.

It was while we were on Key West, prowling around in front of Ernest Hemingway's old house (looking for cats with extra toes), that my phone vibrated.

"Hi," I answered.

Caller ID had already told me that the call was from Dorito, but the voice on the other end of the line let me know that it was actually my seven-year-old granddaughter, Hannah.

"Brinnnnng, brinnnng," she said, imitating the ring of a telephone. This was her standard way of starting conversations with me.

"Hello?" I said, ready to play along.

"Hi," she said. "Is 'I love you' there?"

"I love you?" I asked, feigning confusion.

"I love you too!" she cried and then she began to giggle hysterically. I laughed with her and then she told me the reason for her call: her mom had had a sonogram earlier in the day and her dad was too chicken to call and tell me that she was going to have another sister.

After we came home from Florida, all of our attention turned to Grace and Andrew's wedding. The wedding was going to be in California (which had the potential to turn into a logistical nightmare), but eventually everyone who needed to be there (and, more importantly, all of the dresses and tuxedos) arrived safely on the West Coast. When Marco arranged to have a BMW convertible waiting for him at the airport, Grace complained that he was showing off and trying to steal attention away from *her* on what was supposed to be *her* big day. (I noticed, however, that this didn't stop her from jumping in the front seat when he was offering everybody rides.)

At the rehearsal dinner I was sitting and talking about our upcoming fishing trip with Dorito and Tanner (who – like all of our children – Grace regarded as family and wouldn't have considered having a wedding without), when I suddenly heard her call to her future father-in-law, who was sitting at an adjoining table.

"Yes?" he answered.

"Would you please get my brother for me?" she asked innocently, motioning toward Marco, who was sitting a few tables farther away.

"Oh, no," I muttered, shaking my head. Tanner and Dorito both grinned.

Ever since she was a little girl, Grace's chief objective in life had been to annoy Marco. Whatever she threw at him he usually let roll off his back, but Grace had managed to find one surefire method of getting under his skin.

Everyone who knew the two of them would have answered Grace's request with, "No. Get him yourself!" But Andrew's dad didn't know any better and he promptly turned in Marco's direction.

"Marco?" he called loudly.

"Po-lo!" Grace sang even louder, shooting Marco an evil grin. He actually picked up a salt shaker from his table and threw it across the room at her.

"Hey!" she shouted when it hit her. "You're not supposed to throw things at the bride!"

"Bride of Godzilla!" he shot back. Then he looked at Andrew, who was sitting next to her, and added, "No offense."

I had found out two weddings ago that there is really no good place for the father of the bride to be on the wedding day. The room where the groom is getting ready (in this case, the church's library) held the groom and his buddies and his father and other people who, in general, knew him really well. Having only met Andrew a few times before, I felt like a gatecrasher when I stepped in to speak with him – not really knowing whether I was supposed to wish him luck or just glare at him and threaten him with bodily damage if he ever hurt my little girl. After I finished mumbling something to him, I stepped back out into the hallway and then wandered into the vestibule, peering into the sanctuary that was quickly filling up with people. Marco and Dorito didn't really know Andrew all that well either, so they weren't groomsmen, but they were ushers, and I saw that they were busily seating people who came in from the blistering heat outside.

Finally I moseyed into the parlor where Grace was getting ready. She was fully dressed now and surrounded by her sisters and Laci as they worked on her hair and veil and dress. I sat on a couch and waited for my big moment to arrive.

While I sat there, I thought about the day I had given Lily away and I remembered giving Meredith away, too. Both of them had cried right before I'd walked them down the aisle, and I wondered now if Grace was going to cry, too. (Somehow I doubted it. Grace was a lot like Charlotte – a petite, red-headed Charlotte – fiercely proud and rarely letting anyone see her vulnerable side. But of course, even stoic Charlotte had teared up just before I'd given her away, so I guess you could never tell.)

Eventually Dorito came and got Laci to escort her down the aisle and her sisters lined up in the vestibule, ready to be paired up with the groomsmen and finally I found myself alone with Grace, my youngest daughter.

I looked at Grace, hoping she was going to give me a chance to tell her how much I loved her or something, but she refused to look back at me, instead choosing to check her makeup in the mirror again for the umpteenth time. Then the parlor room door cracked open and Marco stuck his head into the room.

"What are you *doing* in here?" Grace shrieked when she saw him. "You're supposed to be sitting down already!"

"Come here for a minute," he said, beckoning to her.

"Why?"

"Just come out here," he demanded, sounding exasperated.

"What's wrong?" Grace asked, standing up and staring at him with alarm on her face.

"Nothing's wrong," he insisted. "Just *come out here!*"

She cast a glance in my direction and then pursed her lips, stalking to the door that Marco held open for her until she and her dress had made it safely into the hallway.

I eased over to the door and opened it a crack, seeing the two of them just a few yards down the hall. Marco had his hands on Grace's arms and he was talking to her intently. I couldn't hear what he was saying, but I had the feeling he was telling her how much he loved her (even though she had been nothing but abysmal to him since the day we'd brought him home).

Finally Grace gave Marco a nod and he kissed her on the cheek and then they hugged each other. I backed away quickly from the door.

"Everything okay?" I asked innocently when she came back into the room with wet eyes.

She nodded and marched over toward a box of Kleenex that was sitting on an end table.

"Stupid Marco," she muttered, dabbing at her eyes and still refusing to look at me.

"You know, Grace," I ventured, "there's nothing wrong with crying every now and then . . ."

"I do not *want* to cry," she said through gritted teeth, stomping her foot and glaring at me with angry eyes.

"Right," I nodded.

She shook her hair out behind her and checked her veil in the mirror one more time.

"You ready?" I asked.

I held my arm out to her and she nodded, but before she could take it she began to cry in earnest.

"Shhhh. It's okay, Grace," I soothed, rubbing my hand across her back. "I'm very proud of you and I love you so much–"

"Stop it!" she cried, stomping her foot again. "Don't make it *worse!*"

"I'm sorry," I said, deciding to shut up. She dabbed at her eyes again and shook her hair out one more time and then finally took my arm.

"I'm ready now," she declared, nodding at me and then holding her chin high into the air, reminding me once again of Charlotte.

I nodded back at her.

"And," she went on, looking away, "I love you too, but I don't wanna talk about it anymore."

"Right," I agreed again, nodding one more time.

We went out into the hallway and down to the vestibule and then she let me kiss her on the cheek before we entered the sanctuary. As I took Grace's arm and we began to walk down the aisle, I couldn't help but shake my head, wondering if poor old Andrew had any idea what he was getting himself into.

~ ~ ~

SHORTLY AFTER THE wedding, Laci flew to Mexico while Tanner, Dorito, and I headed to Alaska.

We spent a few days fishing for halibut from a charter boat on Resurrection Bay, and after that we drove about an hour inland, where Dorito had reserved a cabin for us at a tremendous resort on the Kenai River.

Someone showed us to our cabin and helped us drag our bags up to it. We were told to take a few minutes to settle in and then come down to the lodge so that we could have lunch.

"This place is fantastic," Tanner said, looking around.

"Yeah," I agreed. "It's great. Good job, Dorito."

He grinned at us as he unzipped his duffle bag. I walked to the door and stood against the frame, listening to the sound of the Kenai River flowing while he and Tanner unpacked.

I watched Tanner as he took a Bible out of his bag and set it down on the nightstand next to his bed. Like he'd told me he was doing months ago, Tanner had been reading his Bible every day. He still refused to talk to me about God, however, and I found it unbelievable that someone could read the Word every day and yet remain so apparently unaffected.

Standing there, watching Tanner, I wondered if maybe – just *maybe* – this trip (with the rushing river and the snow-capped mountains, the bald eagles and the . . . the *grandeur* . . .) would make Tanner realize that simply believing in God wasn't enough – that it was about something more.

I had felt for a long time that God was working persistently in Tanner's life and that it was only a matter of time until Tanner reached out to God, but . . .

122

You need to try to talk with him about it.

This was not the first time that this thought had come into my mind and as it did, I forced myself not to focus on all the other times I'd tried to talk with Tanner about God but had failed.

While we're here. Before you go home.

I needed to.

I knew that I did.

And so I made up my mind that before we left, I was going to have a talk with Tanner.

After we had unpacked, we walked back down to the lodge for lunch. When we arrived, our guide was waiting for us.

Her name was Cora.

She was pretty and maybe ten years younger than Tanner and I. As she introduced herself to us I didn't notice a wedding ring, and I glanced uneasily at Dorito and then at Tanner (who already had a mischievous look on his face).

"Seriously?" I asked Dorito, after Cora and Tanner had set off toward the dining room, already fully engrossed in a conversation and completely ignoring us.

"I . . . I had no idea that we'd get a female guide," he insisted.

"No," I agreed, "you probably didn't. Tanner just magically *draws* women to himself somehow."

Dorito grinned and I managed a laugh, but inside I felt my resolve slipping away. I had a feeling that somehow I was going to have a very hard time keeping the promise I had just made to myself.

Cora spent about an hour working with us on fly-fishing and (even though we were right in front of the lodge where people were practicing their casting techniques all the time) we actually caught a few fish. The best part though, in my opinion, was when a brown bear ambled across the river, upstream from where we were.

We had seen a couple of bears while we were on the charter boat, halibut fishing, but they'd been a long way off. This bear was only about fifty yards away and I stood there, looking at it with my mouth open, until it disappeared into the woods.

I looked at Dorito and Tanner and whispered, "That was awesome!"

They both smiled at me and Cora told me that I hadn't seen anything yet.

After that, Cora drove us a few miles upstream where we got in an hour or so of "real" fishing and saw two more bears. When it started getting dark, Cora drove us back to the lodge for dinner and then advised us to get a good night's sleep.

"You'll want to be rested up for tomorrow," she promised.

Over the next few days we fished some of the upper stretches of the Kanai and took a floatplane to the Nushagak River in Bristol Bay where we fished from a boat and saw a lot more bears. The best part of the trip by far, however, was when we flew in to Big River Lakes.

Big River Lakes (it turns out) is just one lake. It drains into Big River, where it forms swampy areas full of channels to navigate and fish. When we fished these channels we could actually *see* the fish moving beneath the surface, churning up the water as they swam, and more often than not, we caught a fish every time we threw out our lines. We'd caught our limit each day so far, but never as fast as we did while we were at Big River Lakes.

On our last full day in Alaska, we decided to return there, but after we'd landed on the lake and gotten into our boat, Cora surprised me by not heading back to Big River.

"Trust me," she said when I protested.

124

This time we went to Wolverine Creek (which flows into Big River Lakes). There, we were actually fishing *with* the bears, and it was the coolest thing that I'd ever done in my life.

Not surprisingly, when I found that our last evening in Alaska was upon us, I also found that I had not yet managed to talk with Tanner like I'd promised myself I would. We packed our bags before dinner and when Dorito and Tanner finished before I did, they both headed down to the lodge.

Alone in our cabin I resolved – one more time – that I would talk to Tanner.

Over the past few days we had developed a nightly habit of sitting around the huge stone fireplace, enjoying coffee and chocolate fondue, but it was a nice evening and I made up my mind that I would invite Tanner to sit with me out on the deck that overlooked the river.

After dinner, however, I made the mistake of going to the restroom before nabbing him, and when I got back, he was nowhere to be found.

"Where's Tanner?" I asked Dorito.

"He and Cora went off somewhere."

"You have *got* to be kidding me."

"This surprises you?" Dorito asked.

"No," I said, shaking my head and sighing. "It disappoints me."

"Why?"

I looked away.

"What's the matter?" Dorito persisted.

"I . . . I just worry about him," I finally admitted, shaking my head again.

"I really think they're just talking."

"No, that's not what I mean."

"What then?"

It looked like I'd be talking with Dorito on the deck tonight instead of Tanner.

"You wanna go out there?" I asked, pointing outside.

After we settled into chairs and stared at the river for a moment, I finally told him what was on my mind.

"I don't know how much time I have left," I said, looking at him to make sure that he understood what I was saying.

He did.

"And there're some things I'm really worried about," I went on. "I mean, if I could just know some things before I'm gone, it would really give me some peace of mind."

Dorito looked at me for a moment. "What kind of things?" he finally asked.

"Like Tanner," I said, waving my hand in the direction I'd last seen him. "I know he says he believes in God and I know he says he reads his Bible every day, but . . ." My voice trailed off.

"You want to know that you're gonna see him again one day?" Dorito suggested when I didn't finish.

"Yeah," I nodded, relieved that he knew exactly what I'd been trying to get at. "I mean, I think it's gonna happen and everything, but I wanna *see* it happen, you know? I want to *know* that I'm going to see him again one day."

"You might not get to know that," Dorito said gently.

"I know," I said, and I looked away again.

"And all that's really important is that it happens, not that you *know* it happens."

"I know," I said again, sighing.

"What else?"

"Huh?"

"What else are you worried about?"

"Oh," I said.

I looked back at him.

"Amber," I finally answered.

126

This time it was Dorito who looked away.

"I want to see her get married," I told him. "I want to walk her down the aisle like I did with Grace and Meredith and Lily. I want her to have kids. I want to know that she's okay."

"That might not happen either," he said quietly, still not looking at me.

"I know," I agreed. "I'm just telling you what I *want* to have happen."

He nodded and finally looked back at me.

"What else?"

"I want to know somehow that your mom's going to be okay," I said quietly.

"What do you mean?"

"I mean this is going to be *hard* for her," I explained. "I worry about how she's going to be able to handle everything."

He smiled and said with a little laugh, "You don't have to worry about that one! Mom's going to be *fine*."

I looked at him questioningly.

"Dad," he exclaimed, raising an eyebrow at me. "You have *six* kids! Do you honestly think we aren't going to make sure Mom's okay?"

"I just worry about her."

"I know you do," Dorito said, putting his hand on my arm, "but we're going to take care of her."

I nodded, and then I told him, "I want her to move back to Mexico after I'm gone."

"What?"

"The only reason she's in the States is because of me," I told him. "She belongs in Mexico. You know that's where her heart is."

"No," Dorito smiled. "Her heart's with *you*."

"Listen to me," I said, shaking my head. "Even if it's a really long time from now – even if she can't really work anymore – I want you to move her down there with you and take care of her and let her spend the rest of her life down there once I'm gone. That way she can still go to the orphanage and visit and stuff."

"Okay," Dorito nodded.

"I hate to put a burden on you and Maria like that," I said, "but if I just knew she was going to go back there one day . . ."

"It's not a burden," he assured me. "I promise I'll bring her back down there."

I looked at him for a moment and knew he was telling me the truth.

"Thank you," I said, feeling a bit better about one thing at least.

"No problem."

"You gonna drag Tanner to a revival for me?" I smiled. "Make sure that gets taken care of too?"

"I don't know," Dorito said uncertainly, glancing toward the lodge. "I think we just might need some Divine intervention there."

"I just feel like I haven't done what I'm supposed to," I said, shaking my head. "Every time I try to talk to him about God, he always manages to get out of it somehow. I thought that maybe having him trapped here in the Alaskan wilderness would be a good opportunity, but no . . . he's managed to escape yet again." (Of course I had missed plenty of other opportunities through no one's fault but my own.)

"Maybe when you're in Montana?" Dorito suggested helpfully. "When it's just you and him?"

"And Hawk," I reminded him. "Don't forget about Hawk."

(According to Dorito, who had also been in charge of making all of the arrangements for our Montana trip, someone named "Hawk" was going to be our guide while we were elk hunting.)

"Maybe it'll turn out to be a really good thing that I'm not going along," Dorito said. "Maybe having some time alone with him is exactly what you need."

"Maybe," I agreed doubtfully, "but with my luck, *Hawk*'s going to wind up being some unattached, blond bombshell."

~ ~ ~

THREE MONTHS LATER, Laci flew back down to Mexico (to be there when baby Chelsea arrived) and Tanner and I flew to Montana, where I discovered that "Hawk" was not an unattached, blond bombshell – not by a long shot.

Hawk was a scrawny, weathered, old man with a strong drawl, rope-like arms, and enough facial hair to put Grizzly Adams to shame.

He met us at the airport in Billings with a beat-up pickup truck and then drove us to the main hunting lodge at breakneck speeds. The trip took about forty minutes (but I'm pretty sure that if anyone else had been driving – even Tanner – it would have taken at least twice that long). The curvier the roads became, the faster he seemed to go and I kept double-checking my seatbelt. As we swerved along I also kept glancing over at Tanner, wondering if perhaps this near-death experience could possibly be his "coming to Jesus" moment (but unfortunately he actually looked as if he were having the time of his life).

By the time we arrived at the lodge my muscles were so tense and I felt so sick that it was all I could do to crawl from the truck. Tanner bounded out, inhaled deeply, and stretched his arms wide.

"Smell that?" he asked, probably referring to the strong scent of pine and hemlock that was in the air.

"I'm just trying not to throw up," I muttered. Tanner shook his head at me in that disgusted way he had mastered over the years and grabbed his duffle bag and archery case before heading up the steps to the lodge.

The lodge was very impressive and when I saw a hot tub on the deck just off the dining room, I made a mental note to forgive Dorito for the ride I'd just experienced. Hawk took us on a brief tour of the grounds and then showed us to our rooms so that we could dump all of our stuff and "freshen up" before we ate.

Dinner that night rivaled anything I'd ever tasted, even trumping the food we'd had at the lodge in Alaska. Tanner hoped out loud that the chef was going to be accompanying us on our trip.

"I don't think so," I said, shaking my head. "I think it's just you and me and Hawk."

"He's doing the cooking?" Tanner asked doubtfully.

"I think so," I nodded. "But maybe the chef makes everything up ahead of time and Hawk just kind of warms it up once we get out there."

"I hope so," Tanner said, taking a bite of elk tenderloin that the chef had prepared to get us "in the mood for elk hunting" (just in case we weren't already).

"Git some sleep," Hawk advised us after dinner. "We'll ride out first thang in the mornin' and git in ta base camp 'fore chow time tomorrow night. Sound good?"

Tanner and I told him that it did, and he said good night to us as we turned to trudge up the stairs. Once we reached the landing, Tanner looked at me before we went into our separate rooms.

"How are we riding to the base camp?" Tanner asked. " Four-wheelers?"

"I'm not sure," I admitted, casting a worried glance back down the stairs. "I just hope it's not with *him* driving that *truck*."

After a mammoth breakfast in the morning that managed to satisfy even Tanner, the chef put out a tremendous display of foods and told us to pack our lunches.

"Take plenty," he urged us. "Riding'll make you hungrier than you expect."

Tanner took this comment to heart and packed enough food to feed a small squadron of Navy Seals. After the chef had finally managed to fit everything into a cooler, he hoisted it onto his shoulder and set it on the front deck where we had put our gear earlier. I was disheartened to discover that Hawk was loading our things into . . . *the truck*.

"I can't ride with him all day," I whispered to Tanner. Tanner's response to this was to laugh at me. "I'm serious Tanner!" I cried. "I'm going to be sick as a dog by the time we get to base camp!"

"Aww, you'll be fine," Tanner said, pounding me on the back. "Suck it up."

I climbed into the cab and buckled up . . . tight. Hawk started the truck, it lurched forward, and I closed my eyes, trying to remember tips and hints for avoiding motion sickness.

Don't read (as if anyone could actually keep hold of a book as we veered sharply down the road and knocked against one another). *Look straight out the window* (this was difficult to do since the road was so winding that "straight" out the window changed every second or so). *Use acupressure* (I remembered someone once showing me wristbands that you could wear that would prevent motion sickness by putting pressure at a specific point on your wrists).

If I remembered correctly, that specific point was located right where you would slit your wrists (if you were so inclined to do so). I pushed a thumb into that spot on one wrist and then tried to get my other thumb onto the same spot of my other wrist. This was not an easy task and I was fully aware that I must have looked like an idiot.

"What in the *world* are you doing?" I heard Tanner ask (he may not have actually said "world").

" Shut up, Tanner," I replied, and I laid my head back and closed my eyes.

After a fairly short amount of time, the truck slammed to a halt. Certain that we'd hit an elk (or an elephant), I tentatively opened one eye.

131

"Are we at basecamp already?" I asked hopefully, not seeing anything dead in front of us.

"Naw," Hawk said, shaking his head. "We's at the trailhead. Time to saddle up!" And with that he climbed out of the cab and slammed his door shut.

Uneasily I cast a sideways glance at Tanner. He turned slowly and eyed me questioningly.

"*Saddle up?*" he asked.

"I . . . I told Dorito no horses," I stammered. "Maybe that's just a term people use around here for getting on a four-wheeler."

"You'd better hope so."

"Hey!" I cried. "I didn't arrange any of this! This was all Dorito's doing!"

"He's *your* son," Tanner said, opening his door.

There were no four-wheelers anywhere in sight. Just troughs and saddles and reigns and horses.

"Smell that?" I asked after I'd climbed out behind Tanner. I inhaled deeply and stretched my arms wide, just like he'd done yesterday when we'd arrived at the lodge.

"I'm going to kill Dorito," he promised, glaring at me. "I'm absolutely going to *kill* him!"

"Aww, you'll be fine," I promised Tanner, pounding him hard on the back. "Suck it up."

We "saddled up" and if I hadn't felt so sorry for Tanner's horse I probably would have laughed. His horse gave him what I'm sure was a dirty look and Tanner gave him one right back, then I grinned, pressed my heels into my horse's side, and said, "Yee-haw, giddy-up!" and we took off.

After a few hours we stopped for lunch and then continued on. Along the way, Hawk pointed out signs of recent elk activity: a rub where an elk had scraped away the velvet from his antlers and a fresh wallow where an elk had rolled around in the mud to cool off (because apparently the bulls get overheated while trying to find dates). He even showed us where an elk had urinated, explaining to us how he could tell that it had been a female ("Girls splash. Boys stream."). This was almost more information than I needed to know.

Eventually we arrived at our campsite, where a spacious wall tent was waiting for us. We unloaded some of our gear and set off on horseback again, this time to check out a nearby ravine.

Hawk showed us where elk had been traveling lately and why he felt that this area was where we should return in the morning and where we would start and how we would use the bull and cow calls. He let both of us practice and when Tanner was bugling, he actually got a bull to bugle back. It was fairly far off and we couldn't pursue it since dusk was falling, but it was pretty exciting just the same.

That evening, after dinner, we sat around the campfire, watching it slowly fade into embers. The night was clear and the stars were brilliant – their grandeur reminding me of Alaska.

I looked at Tanner, his face illuminated by the dying fire, and I remembered the promise I'd made to myself about getting him alone and talking to him about his relationship with God.

Then I looked at Hawk, who hadn't been more than twenty yards away from either one of us all day, and I wondered how exactly I thought that was going to happen.

We had only been out for about an hour the next morning when we saw a small herd of elk. Through the spotting scope, we determined that one of the bulls was definitely worth our time and then Tanner and I got into an argument about which one of us was going to go for it.

I wanted Tanner to take it because Hawk felt we'd be able to circle around and get close enough for Tanner to get a shot with his bow and arrow. (He'd also brought a rifle and a handgun along, but he wasn't going to use them unless he had to.)

"If we spook it we might screw up the only shot we have all week," Tanner argued. "I'd rather get some meat in the freezer first and *then* we can work on getting up close."

I was finding that dealing with Tanner these days was a lot like dealing with Laci. Both of them spent all their time and energy trying to do things they thought would make me happy while at the same time acting like it was what they really wanted to do. I knew the real reason Tanner wanted me to take this elk was because he had a lifetime of opportunities ahead of him, but this might very well be my only chance.

Now that I'd caught on, however, I decided two could play at that game. I looked at Hawk, who shrugged at me, and then I agreed to take the shot. I figured if I got my elk now, then we'd still have three full days left to work on getting Tanner one.

The wind was in our faces so we crept as close as we dared until we were about two hundred and fifty yards away. By the time I was set up and ready to go, however, the bull was facing away from me. Tanner rattled some antlers and piqued his interest and when he turned broadside to see what all the commotion was about, I dropped him.

He was a nice bull, with six tines on one side, seven on the other, and a decent spread. We field dressed him, carted him back to camp, quartered him, and took care of the meat and hide, and then it was time for lunch.

The area where I'd taken my elk had now been disturbed. Unlike whitetails, Hawk explained while we ate, elk are not territorial. We had spooked the herd out of that area and they wouldn't be back. It was time to find new hunting grounds.

We found not only new hunting grounds, but fresh signs and huge tracks as well. We also found a urine stream, which Hawk assured us had been made by a large bull. (I don't know how he thought he could tell – I contended that maybe it was a *small* bull who had just had a lot to drink – but he seemed pretty confident.) By dusk we'd only seen two cows, however, and Hawk said we should come back the next day.

"I thought they weren't territorial," I said.

"They ain't," he agreed, "but if they got a good spot and don't get spooked they'll keep comin' back day after day. He's got good cover and a food source and water . . . trust me – he'll be here."

The next morning we were up early and we returned to the place where we had last seen signs of (what Hawk had now become convinced was) a monster bull. Sure enough, fresh signs appeared over and around the ones we'd seen yesterday and the tracks he'd left in the newly fallen snow convinced me and Tanner that he was a monster bull too.

Finally I sighted him through the spotting scope about a mile away, at the top of a meadow, grazing quietly with two cows. I showed him to Tanner, who whistled quietly through his teeth and could not suppress a smile.

"Well, well," I smirked. "No wonder you were so anxious to pass on that elk yesterday."

A look of concern crossed Tanner's face before he realized I was joking and then he grinned.

If the elk stayed anywhere close to where it was, there was a very good chance that Tanner would be able to work his way out into the nearby timber and take it with his bow. Since the wind was in our favor, we decided to ride in a big loop to the other side of the wood and hope that Tanner would be able to sneak close enough to take it.

We turned our horses around and set off.

A branch was digging into my neck. I stepped away from it and reached my hand up to my neck to rub it gingerly.

Hawk was a few yards away, on his horse, looking at me. Tanner, who was off his horse and holding his rifle, was looking at me too.

"What's wrong?" I asked, still kneading my neck. Tanner had a look about him that I'd never seen before. He was pale, shaking, and had a frantic expression on his face.

It took me a moment, but I realized that Tanner was scared. I tried to remember if I had ever seen Tanner scared before in my entire life.

I finally decided that I hadn't.

I looked over my shoulder, half expecting to find a bear towering over me with saliva dripping from its jaws. There was nothing behind me except for my horse and a ponderosa pine. I turned back to Tanner.

"What's going on?"

"Nothing," he said. "Everything's great." He swallowed hard and turned away, putting one foot in a stirrup and hoisting himself up onto his horse.

I turned back to my horse and started to do the same when I suddenly realized I didn't have my rifle. I turned back to Tanner and looked at him carefully, finally understanding that he hadn't been holding his rifle, but mine.

"Why do you have my gun?" I asked him, taking a few steps toward him.

"I've just got it," he said, slinging it over his shoulder.

"Why?" I asked again.

He glanced uneasily at Hawk and then looked back at me.

"I just do, okay? Now get back up there and let's get going."

His voice quavered and his hands were still trembling. He squeezed his heels to start his horse forward, but I reached up and grabbed her rein before he got started.

"What's going on, Tanner?"

"Nothing," he said, shaking his head. "Everything's fine."

"Obviously not," I said. I glanced at Hawk, who continued to stare at both of us, poker-faced. "What happened?"

"Everything's fine," Tanner insisted, reaching forward and removing my hand from the rein. "Now let's get moving."

He pressed his heels into his horse's side again, shook her reins, and made a little clicking sound with his mouth. She took off at a brisk walk and Hawk followed on his horse.

"Can I have my gun back?" I called after him, but he didn't answer.

When they were both about thirty yards away they finally stopped and turned around to stare at me. I had little choice but to catch up. I hopped up onto my own horse and started after them.

It soon became obvious that we were no longer stalking a monster elk, but were instead headed back to camp. When we arrived, Tanner dismounted and didn't even take the time to secure his horse to the hitching post. He stalked off into the woods, muttering something about going for a walk. He still had my rifle with him.

I dismounted too and took the reins from both horses and hooked them over the post.

"What happened?" I asked Hawk as we started unbuckling saddles.

"I dunno," Hawk shrugged, trying to act nonchalant. "You got a little bit . . . upset, that's all."

137

"Upset," I repeated.

Hawk nodded.

"Would you just *tell me* exactly what happened?" I asked. "What did I do?"

Hawk undid another buckle and lifted a saddle before he answered me.

"Ya was behind us," he finally said. "Didn't notice right away, but ya'd stopped . . . got off yer horse. We kept goin' fer a minute or so – when we saw ya weren't there, we turned 'round and went back. It was like it scared ya – seein' us comin' at ya like that outta the woods. Don't think ya knew who we were for some reason."

"What did I do?"

"Told us to get back," Hawk said. "Said ya didn't want us comin' no closer to ya."

"Did I have my rifle out?" I guessed.

Hawk nodded.

"Did I point it at you?" I asked in alarm. "Did I try to shoot you?"

"Not me," Hawk said matter-of-factly.

"Tanner?" I cried. "I tried to shoot Tanner?"

"Well," Hawk shrugged, "ya said ya were gonna."

"Oh, man," I said quietly, shaking my head. "No wonder he looked so scared."

"Naw," Hawk said, shaking his head. "That ain't what scared him."

"What scared him then?" I asked quietly, almost afraid to find out.

"Well, he hopped down off his horse, purty as you please, and jus' started walking right up to ya, tellin' you that you weren't gonna be shootin' nobody and that ya needed ta give him that gun."

"And then what?" I breathed.

138

"Then ya turned it on yourself – told him if he didn't get away from ya that ya was gonna blow your brains out. *That's* what scared him."

"How did he get my rifle?" I was almost breathless.

"He talked ya out of it," Hawk shrugged. "I dunno exactly, but he just started talkin' to ya real nice and easy like and reasonin' with ya, and purty soon ya set it down on the ground like he'd been tellin' ya to and then ya started backin' away. He picked it up and just kept on talkin' to ya, and that's when it was like ya just kinda came outta it."

He picked up a brush and started to currycomb one of the horses. I started to reach for a brush, too, but he waved me away. I heard leaves rustling behind me and realized that Tanner was back.

"I got it," he assured me as I looked to where Tanner was emerging from the woods. Tanner ignored me and wordlessly headed into the tent with a lantern.

"Okay," I agreed quietly. "Thanks, Hawk."

He nodded and I knew he was going to make himself scarce. I followed Tanner into the tent.

He was sitting on the edge of the cot, staring at the blank wall of the tent. He didn't acknowledge that I was there.

"I'm sorry," I said.

He dropped his face into his hands and shook his head.

"I'm ruining our trip," I went on.

"This isn't about the trip!" Tanner cried angrily, whipping around to face me. "This doesn't have anything to do with the *trip!*"

He turned back away from me and covered his face with his hands again.

"I'm sorry," I said again.

"Oh, my God," he said, a sob escaping him, "I thought you were going to kill yourself."

Tanner knew better than to take the Lord's name in vain around me, but I didn't say anything about it. Instead I stood there, unable to believe that Tanner was *crying*. I'd never seen him cry before.

"I can't believe I almost let you do that," he whispered, shaking his head.

"You didn't almost let me do anything!" I said. "It's not your fault. How were you supposed to know I was going to pull something like that?"

"I should have known," he said quietly, still not looking at me. "You've been . . . you've been getting worse. You haven't been yourself. I wondered if you should be carrying a rifle or not, but then I convinced myself that it was okay because . . ."

"Because why?" I asked when he didn't go on.

"Because I *wanted* it to be okay," he said finally. "I knew it wasn't a good idea, but I let you do it anyway."

"It's not your fault," I said again, but he shook his head and I knew I wasn't going to convince him. I walked around the end of the cot and sat down next to him.

"I've been getting worse?" I asked.

He nodded.

"Since when?" I asked.

"I first noticed it when we were in Alaska," he told me.

Three months ago.

I nodded even though he still wasn't looking at me.

"Worse how?" I asked.

"Just . . . there've just been times when you don't know what's going on. Times when you're obviously not yourself. One time you didn't know where we were . . . you didn't know who Dorito and I were. You get confused, but then it's kinda like you wake up or something and then you come back."

"Dorito knows about this?" I asked quietly.

He nodded at me.

"Does Laci know?"

He nodded again.

"Did you tell her about what happened in Alaska?" I asked. "Or has she been noticing it too?"

"Both."

I closed my eyes, trying not to get mad at all three of them for keeping this from me.

"Why didn't you tell me?" I finally asked.

"I . . . I guess I just wanted it to work," he said, glancing at me. "I wanted you to have a good time."

"I am," I assured him. "I'm having a great time."

He nodded slightly and said, "Good."

It was quiet in the tent except for the sound of the lantern hissing. I knew that Hawk was on the other side of the campsite, taking care of the horses or something.

Tanner and I were alone.

His defenses were down.

I might never have another chance.

"Ya know, Tanner," I said. "I'm not afraid of what's happening to me. I know that God's in control and—"

"Don't even *try* to have this conversation with me," he interrupted sharply.

I didn't answer.

"Trust me," he said bitterly. "The last thing you wanna do right now is try to talk to me about *God*."

I'd never heard him sound so angry before and I knew our conversation wasn't going to happen tonight either.

I sighed.

"I'm sorry I screwed up you getting that elk today," I finally ventured.

"Don't worry about it," he said. "I've got two more days to get something."

"Yeah," I agreed.

"I'm just glad you're having a good time," he went on, the bitterness almost gone from his voice.

"I am," I assured him again. "Well, except for the whole 'trying to shoot people with loaded rifles' thing."

He almost gave me a smile.

"Can you imagine how mad Laci would have been if I'd killed myself?" I laughed.

"She never would have talked to me again," he said, suddenly serious again.

"Aw, don't worry about it," I said, waving my hand at him dismissively. "She never would have talked to me again either."

The next day was completely unproductive. We saw no new signs, sighted nothing through our spotting scopes, and only heard bugling that was coming from at least two miles away.

By the next afternoon – our last day – when we were sitting in the timber eating sandwiches and jerky, I had pretty much accepted the fact that Tanner was going to be going home empty-handed and that it was all my fault.

That's when we heard a limb snap.

We all looked up at one another, suddenly alert. Hawk pulled a cow call out of his jacket pocket and motioned for Tanner to get ready.

Tanner got ready, but it took a lot of cow calling and antler rattling and bush raking before Hawk finally figured out what the big guy wanted.

He wanted a fight.

Once Hawk pulled out a fighting whine call, our monster bull came tearing through the brush at us so fast I barely had time to hiss a desperate whisper at Tanner: "Don't miss!"

He didn't.

We flew home satisfied, and when we landed I turned on my phone and got the message from Laci that baby Chelsea had been born at about the same time we'd boarded our plane in Billings.

"Dorito could have come with us just fine," I told Tanner as we got into his truck in long-term parking. "He hardly would have missed anything."

We drove home in relative silence but when we were a few miles from Cavendish I turned to Tanner.

"This has been great," I told him. "That's something I've always wanted to do."

"Yeah," he agreed.

"I hope you had fun, too."

"I did," he assured me.

I looked at him skeptically.

"I did!" he insisted. "It was great."

"I've done almost everything on my bucket list," I went on.

He nodded.

"*Almost*," I reiterated when he didn't say anything.

That caught his attention.

"Almost?"

"Almost."

"What else do you want to do?" he asked.

"I want to go one more place with Laci," I said.

He nodded again.

"But," I ventured, "I don't think we should go there alone."

There was a long pause.

"What do you mean?" he finally asked.

"I mean we would need *someone* to go with us."

"*Me?*" he asked.

"If you're up for it . . ."

"Up for what? Where?"

"I mean, I can't take her alone," I hedged. "Not this place. Especially not after what just happened."

"Where do you want to go?" he asked again.

"There won't be any guns involved this time!" I promised, adding, "well, at least *we* wouldn't have any guns . . ."

"Where?" he asked, losing his patience. "*Where* do you want to go?"

I glanced away, took a deep breath, and then looked back at him hesitantly.

"Israel," I finally told him. "I want to go to the Holy Land."

~ ~ ~

THE FIRST THING I did when Laci got home was to complain that she and Tanner and Dorito shouldn't have been keeping things from me.

"You should have told me," I said. "As soon as you guys knew that there were problems you should have *told* me so that I could go see Dr. Keener and let him know what was happening."

She nodded at me reluctantly and promised that it wouldn't happen again.

I almost believed her.

After that we made an appointment with Dr. Keener and drove to Minnesota the next week to see him. He didn't seem surprised to find out that I'd become symptomatic again, and he wrote me a new prescription that would double the number of blue pills I'd be taking every day.

"This is the maximum dosage allowed for Coceptiva," he said, making it a point to look at me in a significant way as he spoke.

I nodded to let him know that I got it.

Once this quit working, things weren't going to be such smooth sailing anymore.

The next day I asked Laci to drive me to Southern's – the only Big and Tall Men's Shop in Cavendish and the only place that Tanner shopped for clothing.

"Can I help you?" a young salesman asked, looking me over dubiously after we'd entered the shop.

"I hope so," I said. "I was hoping to get the measurements for one of your customers."

He looked at me even more skeptically.

"We want to order a custom-made jacket for him out of elk hide," Laci quickly explained. "But we want to surprise him, and he shops here all the time so we were hoping maybe you would have the measurements for him."

The outfitter had handled all of the game care for us during our trip. We'd both wanted the meat and the antlers, of course, but Tanner said he wasn't interested in paying to have the entire head mounted or to have the hides tanned. I had pulled Hawk aside and quietly told him that we did want the hides. I figured it was the least I could do for Tanner after I'd almost killed him (or myself . . . or whatever it was that I'd almost done).

It was going to be a couple of months before the hides were ready, but the tannery told me to send them the measurements as soon as I could. Apparently "giant sized" wasn't good enough – they actually wanted some real numbers.

"What's his name?" the salesclerk now asked us.

"Tanner Clemmons," Laci said.

"That's not ringing a bell," he said. "What's he look like?"

"He's about this tall," I said, holding my hand way over my head, "weighs about two-seventy . . ."

The salesman raised an eyebrow at me.

"Everyone who comes in here looks like that!" Laci said, rolling her eyes at me. She pulled out her phone and scrolled for a minute until she found a picture of Tanner. She held it up for the clerk to see.

"I don't recognize him," he said, shaking his head, "but I've only worked here for a few months.

"Can you check your records?" Laci asked.

"Sure," he agreed as he headed over to his computer. As we started to follow him, I spotted another salesclerk.

146

Now Tanner only looked for two things in a potential date: 1.) pretty and 2.) female. This salesclerk happened to meet both of these criteria and I nudged Laci, giving her a meaningful look as I nodded in the woman's direction. Laci looked toward her too and then gave me a knowing smile.

"Excuse me, miss?" Laci called, holding up her phone and walking toward her. "Do you know this man?"

"Oh, that's Coach," the saleswoman said as soon as she saw the picture.

"Is he in the computer?" our original salesman asked, touching the screen.

"Yes," she nodded. "Tanner Clemmons."

"We need his measurements," Laci explained to her as they walked over to the counter to join us.

Soon we had a printout full of huge, astronomical numbers on which the saleswoman made a few changes in pen.

"His arms only measure thirty-nine," she told us (*only?*), "but he likes it when the fit's a little longer. Add an inch here, trust me."

We took the printout home. I started sending the measurements to the tanning company, but I worried that it wasn't going to be right. Maybe I should have just *told* Tanner what I was doing and gotten the measurements directly from him instead of trying to surprise him. Laci assured me that the saleswoman had known what she was doing and that the jacket was going to be absolutely perfect.

Somewhat placated, I turned back to the computer and tried to decide what color to have the hide tanned: chocolate, black, palomino, tobacco, or saddle.

Suddenly I realized that Laci . . . was crying.

"What's wrong?" I asked, walking across the room to where she was standing.

Her hands were over her eyes and her shoulders were shaking.

147

"What's wrong?" I asked again, gently rubbing her arm. "Why are you crying? Please . . . talk to me!"

She ignored me and kept crying.

"Laci . . ." I said softly.

At the sound of her name she looked up at me in surprise and flung her arms around me.

"Oh, David!" she cried, burying her face into my chest.

"What happened?" I asked, hugging her back.

"You didn't know who I was!" she exclaimed, looking up at me.

"I forgot your name?" I asked.

"No," she said, shaking her head. "It wasn't just that you didn't know my *name* . . . you didn't know who I *was*! You didn't have any *idea* who I was!"

"Laci," I said, looking at her doubtfully.

"I'm serious, David," she said, calming down a little now that I apparently *did* know who she was. "You didn't know who I was or that we were married or anything!"

"I'm sorry," I told her, rubbing her back.

"Sometimes before I've felt like maybe you didn't know, but this time I knew for sure . . . it was like you were just *gone*!"

"I'm sorry," I said again.

"No," she said, shaking her head. "It's not your fault. I'm sorry I got so upset."

"Did I take my pills this morning?" I asked. She nodded. "Are you sure?"

She nodded again.

"We *just* increased the dosage," I reminded her. "It probably just hasn't kicked in yet."

She nodded at me one more time and wiped a tear away. I pulled her close and gave her a hug, kissing the top of her head.

That night – when I took my medicine – I held the bottle up and stared at it for a long moment.

Please don't fail me now, I implored the little blue pills. *I'm going to go to Israel.* I shook the bottle as if hoping to make them pay attention and then I mentally said it again. *Please . . . don't fail me now.*

All the kids made it home to Cavendish for Christmas that year, Chelsea meeting most of us for the first time. Lily announced that she was expecting again and I promised her that if she had a *boy* I would buy her a car or take her to Hawaii. I was only kidding, of course, but Grace looked at Andrew and told him that they ought to think about starting a family.

All of the kids were worried, *really worried*, when we told them that we were going to Israel.

"I don't think this is a smart thing for you guys to do, Dad," Dorito said as Marco and Meredith murmured their agreement.

But then as soon as they found out that Tanner was going with us, it quickly turned into a *great* idea.

Suddenly every one of them couldn't have been happier.

Laci was as excited as I'd hoped she would be and she spent hours poring over travel guides and even a lot of time online, planning out what we would do for each of the seven days that we were going to be there.

By the end of March, we were ready to go.

~ ~ ~

OUR FLIGHT HAD three legs. The middle one – from Chicago to Madrid – was, by far, the longest. It was at the beginning of this flight (when we were staring *fourteen* hours of flying time in the face) that Tanner, for the first time, started asking for details about our trip.

"I sent you the itinerary," I said.

"Do you know how many messages I get every day?" he asked.

I reached into my jacket pocket and pulled out some papers, thumbing through them until I found the one with our schedule. I handed it to him.

"Day one . . . Western Wall," he muttered to himself. "Day two . . . Rachel's Tomb. Day three . . . Sea of Galilee."

His eyes quickly scanned the page. "Where's the Dead Sea?" he asked.

"We can go there on the last day," I told him.

"It says 'Open'."

"Right," I nodded.

"Why's it say that?"

"Well, ya know," I said, shrugging. "It means we can do whatever we want."

"Why didn't you just write 'Dead Sea' on there?" he asked.

"Well," I said, "we might decide we want to do something else."

"Don't we want to go to the Dead Sea?"

"Probably," I said, shrugging again, "but you never know . . . something else might come up or we might enjoy something so much the first time that we want to do it again."

"But that's the *only* thing I told you I want to do while we're there," he said, anger creeping into his voice.

150

"I know," I said. "Don't worry . . . I'm sure we'll get to it."

He glanced back down at the paper. "I notice all the things that *you* two want to do are actually on the list," he said crossly.

"Relax, Tanner," I said. "We'll go to the stupid Dead Sea. If we have to we'll give up going to see where Jesus was baptized . . . or where He was born!" I rolled my eyes at him. "All so you can finally *float.*"

"Don't do me any favors," he muttered, thrusting the paper back at me and dropping it into my lap. Then he rested his head back against the headrest and pretended to sleep.

What a grump.

Laci spent the rest of the trip shooting me dirty looks that were intended to make me be nice to Tanner, but I ignored her and he stayed grumpy until we arrived in Tel Aviv.

Not knowing any better, Laci and I allowed ourselves to get separated when we went through security. Suddenly I found myself standing in front of a gruff-looking security guard who was wielding an Uzi.

He looked at my passport and then looked intently into my eyes.

"Who are you?" he asked in a heavy Hebrew accent.

"David Holland."

"Are you Jewish?" he asked.

"No, sir."

"Then why are you here, David Holland? Why do you come to my country?" The way he was staring at me was completely unnerving.

"I'm a tourist," I explained. "I'm here to visit the Holy Land."

"The Holy Land?" he asked. "Where you from?"

"Mexico City," I told him.

He looked at my passport again.

"I mean the United States," I said hastily.

"Why do you say Mexico City?"

"I . . . I forgot," I said. "I used to live there. I forgot."

"You *forgot?*" he asked incredulously. "How do you forget where you live?"

"I lived there for a long time," I explained, licking my lips nervously.

"How long did you live in Mexico City?"

"Twenty years."

"What model of car do you drive?"

"What?"

"Car. Car! You have a car, no?"

I nodded.

"What model is this car?"

I glanced to my left, looking for Laci. She was through security already and was standing behind a barrier a long, long way from me.

I looked back at the guard.

"What model is your car?" he asked again, staring at me relentlessly.

"I . . . I don't know," I finally said.

"You don't know?" he asked.

"I . . . I can't remember."

He turned and looked at another guard who was standing nearby and spoke to him in Hebrew. The other guard walked over to us.

"You come with us," he said, reaching down and taking hold of my arm. As I stood up, I heard a commotion behind me.

"Leave him alone," Tanner's voice called as I was being led away. I turned in time to see two guards grab Tanner by the arms. He yanked free and two more guards advanced.

"In here," one of my guards said to me, giving me a little push toward an adjoining room. I searched around for Laci again but could no longer see her, and then I cast a desperate glance back toward Tanner. He stared at me, unmoving . . . no longer struggling against the guards who had surrounded him.

152

Probably because the muzzle of an Uzi was pressed tightly against the underside of his chin.

I was taken into what I assumed was an interrogation room. Telling them I lived in Mexico City and forgetting what kind of car I drove was nothing compared to the mess I made of things once I was separated from Laci and Tanner and locked in a room with three armed guards firing questions at me one after another. The more worried I became about Laci and Tanner, the less I was able to focus on their questions. I was barely able to answer anything that they asked.

After a few minutes, however, a knock came at the door and a fourth guard stuck his head in the room. After a brief discussion in Hebrew, one of the guards looked at me.

"You are free to go," he said, pointing toward the door.

"I can leave?" I asked.

"Yes, yes," he said, nodding toward the door. "Go on from here. We have more people to ask questions. Go out."

I stood up slowly and cautiously, having this horrible feeling that I was misunderstanding him. I took a tentative step toward the door, praying they weren't going to level their rifles at me if I really did try to leave.

"Thank you," I said quietly, nodding apologetically. I walked toward the door, quickening my pace as I went. Once I got out of the room I immediately saw Laci. She was sitting in a chair against the wall and she stood up when she saw me, rushing to my side.

"Are you okay?" she asked.

I nodded. "Are you?"

She nodded back.

"Where's Tanner?"

"In there," she said, nodding toward another room a few doors down from where I had been. She took me by the hand and led me to where she had been sitting. We each took a seat.

"I'm sorry," I said, looking at her.

"It's not your fault," she assured me, shaking her head. "I told them what was going on and they believed me. They went right in and got you."

"Did you tell them Tanner's with us?"

"Yes," she nodded, "but he got kind of . . ."

She sighed and rubbed her forehead. She looked exhausted.

"You know how he is," she finally said. "They weren't going to put up with anything from him."

"But you told them he was with us?"

"Yes!" she said irritably. "I already told you."

I shut up.

We sat quietly for about ten more minutes and finally the door to the room where Tanner had been taken opened up. Two guards came out, followed by Tanner. Laci and I stood up as he approached. He refused to look at us.

"Are you okay?" Laci asked anxiously.

He ignored her.

"Tanner . . ." she pleaded and he finally glared at her. Next he glared at me, and then he stalked out of security without saying a word to either one of us.

We found a driver and I handed them the address of the hotel we were going to be staying at, and then we took our places in the van. I let Tanner sit up front and Laci and I sat in the back.

"How long before we get to the hotel?" Tanner asked the driver.

"One and a half hours," he answered.

Tanner put his head back on the headrest, closed his eyes, and pretended to sleep again.

In about an hour I leaned forward to get Tanner's attention.

"Hey," I said, smacking him on the shoulder.

He opened his eyes and turned his head to glower at me.

"What?" he growled.

"There's your stupid sea," I told him, motioning out his window. That got his attention and he looked out the window toward the Dead Sea, which was barely visible off in the distance. He didn't pretend to sleep anymore, but stared at it intently, craning his neck whenever buildings got in the way.

"It's pretty," Laci mused.

"Yeah," I agreed.

Tanner didn't say anything, but Laci looked at me and we both smiled at each other.

We got closer and closer and then – when we had almost reached the sea – turned and drove along, parallel to the coast, for about ten minutes. Eventually our car slowed and we turned in to the gated parking lot of a sprawling, ten-story, waterfront hotel.

When the driver parked and Tanner finally realized what was going on, he turned around to stare at me with his mouth half open.

"You're kidding," he finally managed in a hoarse voice.

"I think I did it," I told Laci, smiling and not taking my eyes off Tanner. "I think I've *finally* surprised him."

"I think you're right," Laci laughed.

He stared at me for another moment but then quickly recovered, saying, "You surprised me one other time."

"When?" I chortled skeptically as the driver turned off the car.

Tanner reached for the door handle but glanced back at me before getting out of the car.

"When you talked *her*," he said, nodding toward Laci, "into marrying you."

Twenty minutes later I rapped on the door to Tanner's room. It was three o'clock in the afternoon – Israeli time. He opened the door and let me in.

"Everything to your satisfaction, sir?" I asked, giving him a little bow.

"It's . . . it's unbelievable," he admitted contritely, gesturing to his balcony. "Do you guys have this view too?"

"As if I'd give *you* a room with a view and not get one for us," I scoffed.

"It's unbelievable," he said again.

I grinned at him and we walked to the balcony where we stood at the rail, gazing out at the beautiful water. "Ready to go float?" I asked.

"Is that really okay?" he asked hesitantly. "I mean, what's on the schedule for the rest of the day?"

"Now see," I scolded, "if you had looked *closely* at the itinerary then you'd *know* what was on the schedule for the rest of the day!"

"I'm sorry," he mumbled. He couldn't have looked more repentant if he'd tried.

I studied him for a moment and then decided out loud, "I'm not going to try to surprise you anymore."

"What?" he asked, looking at me questioningly. "Why?"

"I don't like this apologetic, reticent you," I explained. "I want the old Tanner back."

"The *old* Tanner?"

"Yeah," I nodded. "You know – the swaggering, arrogant, smug, self-satisfied–"

He tilted his head at me and raised an eyebrow. Then he raised a finger.

"There he is!" I said, giving Tanner a grin. "That's the one."

"So why are you so excited about floating?" Laci asked on the elevator ride down to the lobby.

"Because I've never floated before," he explained.

"What do you mean, you've never floated before?" she asked.

"I mean I can't float. Whenever I get in the water I sink like a rock."

"He thinks it's because he has no body fat," I told her, rolling my eyes.

"It is!" he insisted. "Body fat's what makes you float and I don't have any. That's why I sink."

I rolled my eyes again and Laci said, "That must be why I float so *well*."

"No," he told her as the elevator slowed to a stop. "You float because you have boobs."

I glared at him.

"What?" he asked innocently. "She does!"

"Thank you!" I said, giving him a shove toward the opening doors as Laci laughed. "I noticed!"

"Yeah," he nodded. "I noticed too."

"So let me clarify here," I said as we left the lobby and walked past a clear, shimmering pool. "Your theory is that the only reason I can beat you in swimming is because–"

"Because I have to expend so much energy just trying not to sink," he finished for me. "If all I had to worry about was going forward like you do . . ."

"Uh-huh," I said.

"If I really do float while we're down here," he said, pointing at the water, "I'll prove it to you."

"You mean like a race?" Laci asked.

"Yeah," he nodded.

"I don't think that's going to work," she said, shaking her head.

"What d'ya mean?" he asked.

"Everything I've seen online says that you can't really swim here . . . all you can do is float."

"Online?" Tanner said in disbelief. "You actually went online?"

"She's been very excited about this trip," I told him and she smiled.

"Obviously," he said, shaking his head. "I never thought I'd see the day when she voluntarily used a computer."

"Oh, come on," she said, smiling. "I'm not *that* bad!"

"Yes, you are," Tanner and I said in unison.

"So I don't understand how all you can do is float," Tanner said. "I mean, you're floating in water . . . you've gotta be able to swim."

"I don't know," she said, shrugging. "I just know everyone says you can't really swim."

By now we had reached the beach. We stopped and looked up and down, searching for a place to put our towels. The beach was a private one – owned by the hotel – and there were oversized umbrellas and chaise lounges scattered all around for us to choose from.

"How 'bout there?" Tanner suggested, pointing to an empty group of chairs not too far away.

We dropped our towels, stripped down to our suits, and headed toward the water.

"Wait a minute!" Laci suddenly said, startled.

158

"What?" I asked. Tanner and I both stopped and turned around to see what was the matter.

"The beach!" she said, looking down at her water shoes. "It's . . . it's *sand!*"

"Yes, honey," I said condescendingly. "That's what beaches are generally made of."

"No," Tanner said, shaking his head. "She's right. I saw it online too. It's supposed to be made of rocks . . . rocks made of salt. The whole beach is supposed to be salt."

I looked around and then squinted down the shore.

"It's salt down there," I told them. "They must have just made the beach sandy for the tourists."

"Well, I wanna see the salt!" Laci complained.

"We can walk down there and see it," I promised her.

"Now?" Tanner cried. "We have to do it now?"

"No," Laci said, shaking her head. "We can go later. I know you want to *float.*"

"Thank you," Tanner said dramatically.

Several yards out into the water, a dozen or so people were floating. One man was lying flat on his back, having his picture made while reading a newspaper, which was propped open on his belly. Laci and I cast sideways glances at each other and smiled. Then we stopped at the edge of the water and watched as Tanner waded out into the Dead Sea.

After he got about ten yards offshore, he turned around and faced us. Then – with a big grin on his face – he fell backward into the water and . . .

"Whooo-hoooo!" we heard him yell. He lifted his head, looked at us again, and yelled, "I'm FLOATING!"

Laci and I grinned at each other again and followed Tanner out into the clear, warm water.

Laci had been right: you can't swim in the Dead Sea. It was weird, but you really couldn't. It felt as if you were sitting on a noodle – without the noodle.

We laughed and talked, marveling at this new experience, but after a few minutes, Laci and I were ready to get out. She was lamenting the fact that the water burned her legs and underarms from where she had shaved, and I made the mistake of rubbing my eye with a wet hand and learned that that is something you never want to do in the Dead Sea.

We got out and stood on the shoreline, watching Tanner, waiting for him to get out too, but he was in no hurry. As a matter of fact, if we hadn't started complaining loudly, I think he would have fallen soundly asleep, floating in the water.

After a while, however, we finally convinced him to come out and join us at the pool where, before long, all three of us fell sound asleep in our lounge chairs.

The next morning I got up before Laci did and sat down quietly at the hotel desk. When Laci woke up, she found me writing on a small piece of plain white paper.

"Good morning," she said, propping herself up on one elbow. "What are you doing?"

"I'm writing something to put in the Wall." I didn't believe that writing prayers out on a piece of paper and stuffing them into the cracks at the Western Wall made them any more special to God, but it was still something I really wanted to do.

She looked at me for a moment and then asked, "What wall?"

"The *Kotel*?!" I said in disbelief. I mean, honestly, how many walls did she think we were going to visit today?

She sat up in bed and looked at me with great concern etched into her face.

160

"David . . ."

"What?"

She swallowed hard.

"What?" I asked again.

"David – we already *went* to the Kotel."

"No we didn't."

"Yes," she insisted worriedly. "We did. We went there yesterday and spent about two hours."

"The Western Wall?" I clarified.

She nodded slightly.

I looked at her for a moment and she looked back at me. I think both of us were at a total loss for words.

"What did we do?" I finally asked.

"We went there and looked at it and Chayyim told us all about it and showed us the tunnels and everything and then we got to go up to it and touch it . . ."

(Chayyim was the tour guide we had hired for our trip. I hadn't even *met* him yet . . .)

I nodded and then looked down at the paper that I'd been writing on.

"Did I leave a prayer?" I asked, looking back up at her.

"I think so," she nodded, and then I remembered that she wouldn't have been with me when we were actually at the Wall because women and men were kept separated from each other.

"What are we doing today?" I asked. "Rachel's Tomb?"

She nodded and I nodded back. Then I looked down at my paper again, folded it, and looked back at her.

"Come on, get up," I told her, stuffing the paper into my pocket and smiling. "I'm starving."

She looked at me, nodded again slightly, and then got out of bed and headed for the bathroom.

I heard her turn the water on in the tub and I heard it running for a long time, but I never heard her switch the water so that it was coming out of the shower instead of the faucet. I kept waiting for the sound, but it never happened, so eventually I stood up and walked over to the bathroom door and pressed my ear against it, listening.

Laci was crying.

I suddenly remembered, very vividly, when her mom had been diagnosed with stage four breast cancer. For three months, Laci had wrapped her arms around me and sobbed against my chest every day. Usually she would cry for a couple of minutes and then stop, step away from me, and wipe her eyes. I'd brush her hair away from her face and ask her if she was okay and she would say that yes, she felt better. I don't know *why* it made her feel better, but I guess sometimes she just needed to have a good cry because she was losing her mother.

But now she was losing *me* . . . and she was in the bathroom . . . all alone.

I opened the door gradually and peeked in. She was sitting on the edge of the tub – still in her bathrobe and nightgown – with the water running full blast. At the sound of the door she glanced up quickly and then frantically tried to hide her face from me, turning toward the tub.

"I can't get the temperature right," she stammered, pretending to adjust the faucet.

"Laci," I said, walking over to her. She refused to look at me, even after I shut off the water, but she dropped her head and her shoulders heaved in an uncontrolled, silent sob.

"Come here," I insisted, pulling her gently into a standing position. I made her wrap her arms around my neck and then she put her head on my chest and let herself sob.

I hated it when Laci cried – absolutely *hated* it – and I hated it even more this time because I knew that I was the one who was making her cry. But I stood there, dutifully holding her against me, waiting for her to finally stop. And eventually she did, stepping back and dabbing at her eyes with the sleeve of her robe.

162

"I'm sorry," she sniffed.

"Don't be sorry," I assured her, tucking a strand of hair behind her ear and then wiping a tear from her cheek that she'd missed. "Do you feel better now?"

She nodded and gave me a little smile.

"Guess what?" I asked.

"What?"

"I'm still starving."

She made a noise somewhere between a laugh and another sob and smiled a little more.

"Go have breakfast," she urged. "I'll be down in a little bit."

"You sure you're okay?"

"Yeah," she nodded. "I'm fine."

"Okay," I agreed. I grabbed the belt to her bathrobe and pulled her up against me. I stroked her cheek again. Her eyes were red, her face flushed.

"I love you," I said softly.

"I love you, too," she whispered. We kissed for a long moment and then I rested my forehead against hers.

"Are you sure you're okay?"

"Go eat," she said, giving me another quick peck on the lips before she turned me toward the door and patted my shoulder as she steered me out of the bathroom.

I made sure my room key was in my wallet and then I headed out the door and down the hallway toward the elevator. After I pushed the "Down" button I waited for what seemed like a long time.

While I was waiting, I stood there and worried about what I always worried about these days – Laci. I thought about how upset she had just been simply because I'd forgotten one single day. How was she going to handle it when I didn't remember *anything?* When I never knew her name or couldn't remember who I was? When I was slumped in a wheelchair like my dad, drool running down my unshaven chin . . . my eyes vacant?

Who was going to give Laci a place to lay her head and sob, I wondered, when I couldn't do it anymore?

Tanner was already in the dining room – studying his phone intently – when I arrived downstairs. I helped myself to a Kosher breakfast and joined him at the table.

"Good morning," I told him.

"Mmhhh," he nodded, not looking up.

I sat down, silently thanked God for my food, and then looked at Tanner.

"I don't remember anything that happened yesterday," I told him bluntly.

That got his attention.

"What?" He looked up.

"I said, 'I don't remember anything that happened yesterday'."

"What are you talking about?"

"It's a pretty self-explanatory statement," I said, putting some butter on my English muffin.

"None of it?" he cried. "You don't remember *anything* that we did yesterday?"

"Nope."

"I can't believe that," he said, obviously taken aback. "You were . . . it seemed like you were totally yourself yesterday. You knew everything that was going on."

"I don't remember it," I shrugged matter-of-factly, taking a bite of my muffin.

"I can't believe that," he said again.

164

"I forgot my chocolate milk, too," I told him, swallowing, and I got up and went back to the buffet line. When I returned to the table, Tanner pushed his phone toward me.

"Look at the pictures we took yesterday," Tanner suggested.

"Okay."

I swept my hand across the screen while I ate, ushering in one photo after another. There was no doubt about it, I really had been at the Wall yesterday.

"Is that Chayyim?" I asked, pointing to one of the pictures.

"Yeah," Tanner said.

"I don't know what he looks like," I explained, and Tanner didn't answer.

It was surreal, seeing pictures of myself so clearly doing something, but having no memory of it whatsoever. Finally I handed his phone back to him.

"I don't remember it," I said.

He seemed at a complete loss as to what to say.

"Thanks for taking all these pictures, though," I said. "I'm really glad we have them."

He nodded and put his phone away.

"Laci's taking it pretty hard," I told him.

He took a deep breath and let it out and then he pressed his lips together.

"I mean . . . she's better now," I said, "but she was pretty upset."

"I imagine she was," he nodded again. "It was obviously very . . . *important* to you while we were there, and to think that you don't even remember it now . . ."

"It was important to me?" I asked.

He nodded.

"What d'ya mean?"

"I dunno," he shrugged. "You could tell that it meant a lot to you."

"Why do you say that?"

"I dunno," he said again.

"Well, tell me," I insisted. "What happened?"

"You were just very . . . emotional," he said reluctantly.

"I didn't *cry* or anything, did I?"

He looked at me knowingly.

"I cried?!"

He nodded.

I slumped back in my chair.

"Did you cry?" I whispered conspiratorially.

"As if," he snorted.

"Well, no wonder I don't remember anything," I finally said, sitting forward and trying to regain some of my dignity. "I clearly wasn't myself."

"Oh, you were totally yourself," Tanner said, sitting back and picking up his cup of coffee. "I already told you that."

About fifteen minutes later, Laci joined us. She sat down.

"Did he tell you?" she asked, looking directly at Tanner.

"Yeah," Tanner said.

"Yes," I agreed, in case she'd forgotten I was sitting right there. "I told him."

"Well, guess what?" she said, crossing her arms on the table and leaning forward eagerly. "I want to go back there today and–"

"WHAT?!" I cried. "Absolutely not! We're going to Rachel's Tomb today!"

"We don't have to go to Rachel's Tomb," she insisted. "It's just like you said, '*Why do you wanna go see some gate that's guarding someone's bones?*' That's a stupid thing to go see. Let's just concentrate on the places that were important in the Gospel and–"

166

"No!" I said, interrupting her again. "You've always wanted to see Rachel's Tomb" (for some strange reason), "and that's what we're doing today."

"But you've always wanted to see the Wall!" she argued.

"And I *did* see the Wall," I insisted. "I saw it yesterday."

"But you don't even remember it!"

"Tanner showed me the pictures," I said. "I'm good."

"But David," she pleaded, "I really, really want to go back there. I want you to experience it today when you're . . ."

"Not crazy?" I suggested when she hesitated.

"You weren't crazy," she said, "but today you're . . . yourself."

"According to Tanner I was myself yesterday, too."

"Well," she admitted, "you did seem normal . . ."

Tanner looked at me smugly.

"So today I seem normal too," I said. "What's to say that if we go and see it again today that I'm going to remember it any better tomorrow? We could keep going back every day for a year and I might not ever remember it, Laci."

"What if we—"

"Laci?"

"What?"

"Go get some food."

"But—"

"Tanner's been done with his breakfast for about half an hour and I finished about ten minutes ago and now we *still* have to sit here and watch you eat. So go get some food and we can talk about it while you're eating."

"Fine," she sighed, pushing her chair away from the table. As soon as she was gone I turned to Tanner.

"She's always wanted to see Rachel's stupid tomb," I told him. "I'm not going to let her miss that just so we can go back to the Wall."

"Afraid you're gonna cry again?"

" Shut up, Tanner. No! I just want her to get to do what she's always wanted to do–"

"And she wants you to do what you've always wanted to do," he pointed out.

"Which we already did."

"You don't need to remind me," Tanner said. "I'm not the one who forgot."

I smirked at him, then I said, "Help me out here, okay? I mean – I'll admit that I *did* want to see the Wall and everything, but the main reason I wanted to come to Israel is because *Laci's* always wanted to come here. This trip is for *her*. . . not for me. Do you understand what I'm saying?"

He nodded and Laci returned with a blueberry muffin and a cup of coffee.

"I wanna go back to the Wall," she said resolutely.

"Well," I said, "Tanner and I were just talking and we both think that we should go to Rachel's Tomb."

She looked at Tanner, distraught.

"I never said that," he argued.

"What do you think we should do?" she asked him.

"It doesn't matter what Tanner thinks," I interjected. "We've got a plan and we're sticking to the plan. We're going to see Rachel's Tomb today."

"Plans can change," Tanner said.

"You just wanna see if I'm gonna cry again, don't you?" I asked, glaring at him.

"Well, that would be an added bonus," he shrugged.

"Fine," I pouted, sitting back and crossing my arms. "You two sit here and plan everything out for me like I'm already an invalid. But I thought we were doing whatever I want to do. Right now, I wanna go to Rachel's Tomb."

"Oh, quit sulking," Tanner said. "You're both just about so stupid it's a wonder that you ever get anything done without me."

168

Laci glanced at me as Tanner pulled his phone back out and pulled up our itinerary.

"Now," he said, "Friday's open. Seems to me that we'd better go see Rachel's Tomb today since we've already got bus reservations and everything and we haven't even told Chayyim what's going on. Then, tomorrow, we can go back to the Wall. We'll back everything else up one day and then Friday won't be open anymore. Does that sound like a plan?"

We both nodded at him.

"So, you'll get to see Rachel's Tomb," he said to Laci before turning to me, "and you'll get to see your wall."

"As long as I don't forget it again," I added.

"Maybe you'll get lucky," Tanner said, "and all you'll forget is Rachel's Tomb."

We arrived in Jerusalem, where I met Chayyim . . . again. Chayyim was young – probably in his early thirties – and seemed completely unfazed when told that I had Alzheimer's and no recollection of the day before. He reintroduced himself to me and went into a little spiel about himself and his background. He told me that he was a Conservative Jew and explained that he believed the Bible was the divinely revealed Word of God. Although he did not believe that Jesus was the promised Messiah, he specialized in guiding Christians through the Holy Land, was very familiar with our New Testament, and would be able to provide us with accurate and insightful details about areas of significance in the life of Christ and His followers. (Of course I already knew this – that's why I'd hired him. He had been highly recommended by someone from our church in Cavendish who had visited the Holy Land two years earlier.)

After that Chayyim told me about his *yarmulke* (skullcap) and *tallit* (prayer shawl) and then we set off for the bus station.

The station in Jerusalem was full of shops. We arrived about an hour before our bus was scheduled to leave, so we went through security and then shopped until it arrived. When it finally did, we boarded and took a seat.

The bus was not your average bus. It was a big, bulletproof bus – a bus that picked up an armed guard after we'd left Jerusalem and stopped at a checkpoint before we got to the fortress that Rachel's Tomb had been turned into. Once we finally went through the security gate and cruised through the maze of concrete walls, we got out of the bus and walked into the entryway.

"We'll meet you right back here," I said to Laci urgently, pointing to the fountain where Orthodox Jews were washing their hands before going in to pray.

"Okay," she nodded before leaving to walk down into the women's outer chamber.

"She'll be fine," Tanner assured me, as Chayyim led us through a crowded passageway with the other men. "Everybody else here passed through security just like we did, remember?"

"I remember," I nodded. "I'm just . . . I'm just worried about her."

"I know," he said, patting me on the back. "But she'll be fine."

Finally we came to the inner room where we could see the tomb. All around us Jewish men bobbed their heads up and down in prayer – *shokeling*. Ahead, through the crowd, I could see the white structure of Rachel's Tomb.

"Do you want to get closer?" Tanner asked. I knew that he'd get me right up to it if I wanted him to.

"No," I said, shaking my head. "This is Laci's thing, not mine."

Laci's thing.

Why exactly was this "Laci's thing"?

Why, I wondered (not for the first time) did she care so much about coming to this place? I stood there, trying to remember what I knew about Rachel, hoping to figure out just what it was that fascinated Laci so.

It had been Rachel, of course, who – jealous of her sister – had said to her husband, Jacob, "Give me children or I'll die." Jacob became angry with her and told her that it was God who had kept her from having children, not him. Eventually God did give Rachel a child . . . two actually. First, He gave her Joseph – the one whom Jacob loved more than any of his other sons – and then Benjamin – the one whose birth had ultimately caused Rachel's death. Jacob had buried Rachel on the way to Bethlehem and set up a pillar over her tomb.

And now, thousands of people flocked here to pray . . . including many barren women, asking God to bless them and give them babies.

Babies.

Was that what this was about?

I had no delusion that Laci was in the adjoining room, praying for God to miraculously give her a child, but I did wonder if she was in there crying because God had not given us any biological children – at least none that had lived anyway. The thought that she might be in there crying about this bothered me.

"I wish I knew why this means so much to her," I said to Tanner.

He looked over the small sea of bobbing heads and fixed his eyes on the tomb.

"I think it's the romance," he answered.

"The *romance?*"

"Yeah," he nodded. "The romance between Jacob and Rachel."

"I don't think so," I said skeptically, shaking my head.

"You don't know anything about women," he said dismissively. "See, this is why you had to settle for Laci . . . why you've had to spend your entire life stuck with just one woman."

I laughed at him.

He smiled back at me and then went on. "Think about it," he said, seriously. "Jacob sees this Rachel chick – she brings him some water for his camels or whatever – and BOOM!" Tanner clapped his hands together. "Suddenly he's in love.

"Now he loves her so much that he agrees to work for her dad for *seven* years just so he can marry her. So he works and works and works for seven years and then – he wakes up on the morning after their wedding – and finds out he didn't sleep with Rachel at all! He's been totally hoodwinked by this guy and now he's married to her sister, Leah, instead."

I looked at Tanner with my mouth open in surprise.

"So he agrees to work for *another* seven years because he wants Rachel so bad," Tanner went on. "And then he winds up with over a dozen kids and which ones does Jacob love the most?"

I didn't answer him. I was still staring at him in mild disbelief.

"Joseph," Tanner answered himself. "And then – once he thought Joseph was gone – Benjamin."

Tanner seemed to be waiting for me to agree with him.

"Twelve," I said.

"What?"

"You said that he had over a dozen kids, but he had exactly twelve . . . they became the twelve tribes of Israel."

"What about Dinah?" he asked me.

"Oh, yeah," I stammered.

He looked at me smugly.

"I know all about Dinah!" I said.

"Sure you do," he said.

"I do," I insisted. "I just forgot."

"Uh-huh."

"I did!" I argued. "In case you've forgotten, I have *Alzheimer's!*"

He rolled his eyes.

"But anyway," he said, going on, "don't you get it? Don't you see how much he loved her? She was *everything* to him! Nothing meant

172

more to him than Rachel did . . . and once she was gone, nothing meant more to him than her sons."

"That's what women want," he concluded confidently. "They want someone to love them as much as Jacob loved Rachel. They want to feel that they're the most important thing in the world to someone."

Was that really what women wanted?

And, more importantly, was Laci in the other room right now bemoaning something other than the fact that she'd never had any babies of her own?

The next day we returned to the Western Wall and Chayyim, Tanner, and I once again had to separate from Laci.

Tanner and I covered our heads and – as we approached the Wall – he stuck right by my side.

"I'll be fine by myself," I told Tanner.

"Afraid you're gonna cry again?" he asked with a wicked smile. I smirked at him and gave up hoping for a moment to myself.

Then we stepped up to the Wall.

I know that God is always with us, I really do, but at the moment that I reached my hand out to touch the rough stone, I had never felt His presence more.

It overwhelmed me like nothing I'd ever experienced. And suddenly? Suddenly I didn't care if Tanner was with me or not.

I stepped even closer to the Wall and put both hands on the uneven rock. Then I pressed my forehead against it and closed my eyes. The hair on the back of my neck actually stood up and my knees felt weak. Something was fluttering in my stomach.

How had I been here two days ago and I couldn't remember it now?

The experience was so overpowering that it seemed impossible I could have forgotten. It also seemed impossible that Tanner could be standing here right next to me and remain so completely unaffected.

I was probably crying again, but I didn't care. I stayed there, pressed against the Wall and praying, for a long, long time.

Once I stopped praying (and crying), I took the little slip of paper out of my pocket and tucked it carefully into a crack. Most of the cracks were so full of paper that I had to reach way up high to find a spot where it would stick.

Finally I stepped away, disappointed (but not surprised) to find Tanner standing there, looking at me impassively.

"Where did we stand before?" I finally asked him.

"Right around here," he said, shrugging.

"Did I put a prayer in the Wall?"

"Yeah," he nodded.

"Where?" I asked.

"I dunno," he shrugged. "Why?"

"I want to find it," I said.

"You can't find it!" he exclaimed, motioning to the hundreds of prayers that were stuffed into the cracks all around me. "Even if we knew exactly where you put it, it's all covered up with other ones by now!"

I looked at the Wall and realized he was right.

I sighed.

"I wanted to know what I wrote down," I said, shaking my head in disappointment. "I wanted to see what was going on inside my mind."

Tanner was quiet for a minute, then he said quietly, "I know."

"Know what?"

"I know what you wrote down," he said.

"You do?"

He nodded and I looked at him.

174

"You showed it to me," he explained.

"I did?"

He nodded again.

"What did it say?"

He hesitated for a long moment before answering.

"You prayed for Laci."

He didn't go on, but I knew there was more.

"And?" I prompted.

"And for Amber," he said reluctantly.

"And?" I asked again, still looking at him expectantly.

"And for me," he finally admitted.

I held his gaze, eventually nodded, and then we left, keeping our faces toward the Wall as we'd been instructed.

As we backed away, I thought about the note that I had just left.

If nothing else, at least I was consistent.

The next morning I woke up to find Laci still sleeping. I looked at the clock and discovered that we still had almost an hour before we needed to get up, so I put my head back down on my pillow and snuggled closer, waking her up. I closed my eyes again.

"What are you smiling about?" I heard Laci ask me after a moment.

"Nothing," I said, trying to suppress a grin. "I just really like waking up next to a strange woman every morning."

She swatted me and I laughed.

"No, seriously," I said, opening my eyes. "I was just wondering how mad you'd be if I told you that I was really, *really* excited that we were going to get to see the Wall today!"

"Pretty mad," she said, glaring at me.

"Okay," I smiled. "I'll pretend I remember going."

"David–" she said unhappily.

"You know I'm just kidding," I told her.

"I know," she sighed, shaking her head, "but . . ."

"Okay, I'll stop," I promised. Then I assured her, "I remember everything."

She seemed happier and gave me a small smile. I leaned forward and kissed her and when I pulled away she said softly, "I'm so glad we're here."

"Good," I said, giving her a smile back.

"Are you having a good time?" she asked worriedly.

"Yeah," I nodded. "Absolutely."

"Are you sure?"

"Sure, I'm sure," I said, propping myself up on one elbow. "I'm having a great time. Why?"

"I don't know," she replied. "It just seems like you've been kind of worried or something."

"No," I lied. "I'm not worried about anything."

Actually, ever since we'd gone to Rachel's Tomb, I'd been constantly thinking about what Tanner had told me – about his theory as to why that place had meant so much to Laci.

That's what women want, he'd said. *They want someone to love them as much as Jacob loved Rachel. They want to feel that they're the most important thing in the world to someone.*

This probably shouldn't have bothered me, but the fact was that Tanner and Laci had dated in college

And they hadn't just dated, they had been in *love.*

And one time I had asked Laci what she'd seen in Tanner . . . why she'd ever loved him.

Because he loved me so much, she'd replied.

I had also asked her one time why she loved me, and do you know what she'd said?

Because God told me to.

Because He'd *told* her to. That was her reason.

176

Now I know that marriage is about a whole lot more than just love – it's about honor and commitment and compromise.

And don't get me wrong, it wasn't as if I didn't think that Laci loved me. I had never worried about that.

But who was I kidding?

I worried that Laci didn't realize how much I loved her. That she had no idea how much she meant to me. That she didn't know how grateful I was to God that He had given her to me and that I thanked Him for her every day. I worried that she didn't grasp that – without her – I would have been completely empty and that everything I'd ever had that was worthwhile was because of her . . .

My children . . .
My relationship with God . . .
My life.

I worried that – deep down – Laci somehow felt that she had been gypped.

I looked at her now and ran a finger along her cheek. I brushed a strand of hair from her perfect face and stared into her beautiful eyes.

"You know how much I love you," I asked. "Right?"

She nodded and smiled and I started to nod back, but then I stopped.

"No, you don't," I said, shaking my head. "You have no idea how much I love you because I've never told you."

She looked at me questioningly for a moment and finally said, "Then tell me."

And so I did.

We were late for breakfast.

~ ~ ~

AFTER WE RETURNED from Israel, the little blue pills became less and less effective and the periods of time that I couldn't account for became greater and greater. More and more frequently, I would find myself in the middle of a conversation or an activity that I knew nothing about.

It didn't take long, however, for me to become accustomed to that sensation and I learned that if I quietly observed for a moment or two, I could usually figure out what was going on.

Like when I found myself sitting on a cold, metal bleacher with Laci on one side and Meredith on the other, a blanket stretched across all of our laps.

When you have six children, you cannot have a true "middle child." Instead, Meredith shared this spot with her older sister, Lily. Meredith lived less than two hours from Cavendish with her husband, Danny, their four-year-old, Bianca, and toddler, Zoa.

I looked out onto what was clearly a soccer field filled with young children and searched until I saw a familiar face.

"Go, Bianca!" I yelled when the ball rolled toward her. Out of the corner of my eye, I saw Laci glance at me, surprised. I just looked back at her and gave her a smile.

Bianca gave the ball a swift kick and sent it in what appeared to be the wrong direction. The swarm of children surrounding the ball all moved as one toward the other end of the field. I looked around for a scoreboard, but didn't see one.

"What's the score again?" I asked Laci.

"No one's scored yet," she answered.

"Right," I nodded. I also wanted to know what half it was, but I didn't ask.

178

"Where's Zoa?" I asked, turning to Meredith after a few more scoreless minutes.

"She has an ear infection," she said, looking at me. "Danny stayed home with her."

"Right," I said again. I could tell from the way she said it that I was already supposed to know this, so I added, "I forgot."

Meredith turned her attention back to the game, shouting Bianca's name and clapping her hands. I watched her for a long moment and found myself remembering when I had first laid eyes on her, some twenty-five years earlier.

We'd been at the airport, having just gotten off a plane from Mexico City. Meredith had been almost two at the time and she'd stood quietly, waiting for us to notice her. There had been a tiny ponytail in her hair – sticking straight up out of the top of her head like a wispy, blond palm tree – and she'd held a raggedy stuffed dog tightly in her arms. I remembered that she had come right to us when we'd knelt down not far from her and had spoken her name, keeping that dog clutched to her side (for about five more years) but agreeing to join us as if it was the most natural thing in the world.

I watched her now, her bright blue eyes following Bianca on the soccer field and a strand of golden hair blowing across her face in the gentle, cool breeze.

"Are you happy?" I asked her quietly.

She pulled her eyes away from the game and looked at me.

"What?"

"Are you happy?" I asked again.

She stared at me for a moment and then nodded.

"Yes," she said. "I'm very happy."

"Good," I nodded back.

She gave me a little smile.

"I love you," I told her.

"I love you too, Daddy," she said, giving me a bigger smile and looping her arm through mine. She rested her head on my shoulder and squeezed my arm. A moment later – on the other side of me – Laci did the same thing.

I wondered briefly if we were spending the night with Meredith and her family or if we had only driven up for the day, but I kept quiet, not wanting to ruin the moment by admitting I didn't know. Instead, I just sat between the two of them under the blanket, cheering for Bianca, and deciding that I would just wait and see.

I don't know why I tried to cover up whenever I had no idea what was going on.

Deep down, I think I knew I wasn't fooling anybody, but I guess it just felt good to pretend that everything was normal.

And so when Tanner stopped by after work one evening wearing a new, elk-skin jacket, I didn't let on that I had absolutely no recollection of giving it to him.

~ ~ ~

WE WERE IN the car – just Laci and I.

"Where are we going?"

"To physical therapy."

"I go to physical therapy?" I asked.

"Yes." She sounded tired.

"Why?"

"To keep you healthy."

"Yeah!" I said, pumping my fist into the air. "Let's keep this body going for as long as we possibly can!"

She glanced over at me.

"David?" she asked, questioningly.

"*Laci?*" I said right back in the same tone.

"How are you?" she smiled at me.

"I don't know," I said. "Apparently I'm going to physical therapy, so you tell me."

"You're fine."

"Then why do I go to physical therapy?"

"Your insurance covers it," she shrugged, "so I figured, why not? It's good for you and you seem to like it."

"I've been before?"

"Yeah."

"How many times?"

"A few."

I sighed.

"But I think I'll cancel it for today . . . I'd rather spend time with you."

"Okay," I agreed. We rode along.

"I'm . . . I'm *gone* more now, aren't I?" I asked after a minute.

"Yes," she said quietly, nodding reluctantly.

"How often?"

She hesitated.

"Just tell me, Laci."

"It's kind of hard to tell, but . . . it seems like you're really *here* and aware of what's going on maybe . . . every couple of days."

"When's the last time I was . . . *here?*"

"I think yesterday morning," she said, "but I'm not sure. Like I said, it's hard to tell."

"Why is it hard to tell?"

"Well," she said, "it's not as if some neon sign flashes across your forehead or something saying '*I'm ba-ck!*'."

"Oh," I said. "Well, why do you think I was there yesterday morning? How could you tell?"

"Because you called me 'Laci'."

"That's your name," I pointed out.

"Yes," she agreed, "but a lot of times you don't know who I am. If you call me Laci, I pretty much know that it's you."

"Really?"

"Uh-huh," she answered and I thought for a moment.

"I'm going to use your name whenever I'm talking to you so you'll know I'm really here," I finally decided. "Okay?"

"Okay," she smiled, but I could tell she was skeptical that I'd be able to keep that promise.

"What happened yesterday morning?" I asked.

"Nothing too special," she shrugged. "We had a load of firewood delivered and moved some boxes out of the garage. Do you remember that?"

"I don't think so," I admitted.

"Well," she said, "what's the last thing that you *do* remember?"

"Ummm," I said, trying to think. "I don't really know."

"Do you remember when Lily and Meredith came?" she ventured.

I thought for a minute and then I remembered.

"Yes! And they brought the girls!"

"That's right," Laci smiled.

"And we went to Cross Lake and they fished off of the pier!"

"Exactly."

"And Laney dropped her nachos in the water . . ."

"And she cried and cried," Laci finished for me.

"And we didn't catch any fish."

Laci nodded and smiled.

"When was that?" I asked.

"Last week."

"Okay," I said.

So that's what a week feels like.

We arrived at the hospital and Laci pulled into a parking spot.

"I'm gonna run in and tell them we're not coming," she said. "Stay right here."

"Mentally or physically?"

"Both."

I was still there when she got back.

"Hi, Laci," I said, to let her know. She smiled at me and started the car. I looked at the buildings of the hospital complex. "What do I do in physical therapy?" I asked her as we drove out of the parking lot.

"You work out in the hot tub."

"The hot tub?"

She nodded and smiled at me. "I figured you'd like it."

"Well take me back!" I said. "I don't wanna miss that!"

"They don't let you just *sit* there," she explained. "You have to actually *work* . . ."

"Are you in there with me?" I asked.

"No."

"Well, never mind then," I said. "I'd rather be with you."

She smiled at me again.

"Are you hungry?" she asked.

"Sure."

"You didn't eat much breakfast," she told me.

I looked to see what time it was. My wrist was bare.

"Where's my watch?" I asked her.

"Sometimes you don't want to wear it."

"Really?" I *always* wore my watch.

"Really."

I looked at the clock on the dash.

"That's ten-thirty in the morning, right?"

"Yes," she laughed, "hence all the sunshine."

"Doesn't Hunter's open at eleven?"

"You want a morning meatball sub, huh?"

"Unless you'd rather go somewhere else," I said. "Why don't we go to one of your favorites? Let's go to Jenns. You like their salads."

"No," she said. "Any time you're . . . here, I want to do whatever's going to make you happy."

"But that's not fair," I argued. "That's *my* only chance to make *you* happy!"

"Trust me, David," she said, smiling at me. "You're here with me. I'm happy."

MY DINNER PLATE, full of my favorites, was sitting on the table, apparently untouched. I looked up to find Laci sitting next to me. Her left eye was bloody and partially swollen shut. The skin around it was tight and black.

"WHAT HAPPENED TO YOU!?"

"David?"

"Yes, it's David. What *happened* to your eye, Laci?"

"Oh," she said, reaching up and touching it self-consciously. "It's nothing, really. It was dark and the bathroom door wasn't opened all the way and I just walked right into it, and *bang*. I'm okay. It's nowhere near as bad as it looks."

"Are you sure you're alright?" I asked, reaching over and gently pushing her hair from her face.

"I'm sure," she smiled.

I looked at her uncertainly.

"Eat," she urged. She seemed really happy that I was back.

Reluctantly I started to put my fork into my potatoes.

"Wait," Laci said, taking the plate from me before I could have a bite. "That's probably cold. Let me heat it up for you."

"Why's it cold?"

"I don't think you like it very much," she said, putting it in the microwave and punching a button.

"What do you mean? I love all that stuff."

"*You* love it," she agreed, "but your alter ego is pretty picky."

"My alter ego?" I smiled at her.

"Yeah," she smiled back. "That's who shows up whenever you leave."

"I act different?"

"Oh yeah," she nodded. "You're *completely* different. Kind of like an Anti-Dave or something."

"An Anti-Dave?" I laughed.

"Yeah."

"What's Anti-Dave like?"

"Hmmm," she said, sitting back down. "Where do I start?"

"What do I like to eat?"

"High-fat, high-sugar foods . . . generally anything that's bad for you."

"I've always liked that stuff," I argued.

"Yeah," she admitted, "but at least *you'll* eat *good* stuff too. I'm having a hard time convincing Anti-Dave to eat anything that's nutritious."

"I wouldn't worry too much about it."

"I want to take good care of you," she said in a quiet voice.

"I know you do," I said. "And you *are* taking good care of me, but if I die because I overdose on potato chips and ice cream, that won't be such a bad way for me to go, will it?"

She tilted her head at me and the microwave beeped.

"But, if it'll make you feel better, Regular Dave will eat good right now. Whip me up a couple of Brussels sprouts and I'll even try to choke those down."

She smiled at me and got up, took my plate out of the microwave, and then set it down in front of me.

"So what else is different about Anti-Dave?" I asked, putting my napkin in my lap. "What do I do?"

"You wander around a lot."

"I do?"

"Uh-huh."

"What else?"

"You love watching game shows on TV and playing along with the contestants."

"I do?" I asked her, putting a forkful of potatoes in my mouth.

186

"Yeah."

"Am I any good?"

"Oh, no!" she laughed, shaking her head. "You're awful."

"Tell me something else."

She thought for a moment.

"You ask a lot of questions," she said.

"Like what?"

"Like what day it is, or where we're going."

"Over and over again?" I guessed.

"Sometimes," she admitted.

"You must feel like you're living in an insane asylum," I said, shaking my head.

"Not at all," she smiled, laying her hand on my face and stroking my cheek gently with her thumb.

I put my fork down on my plate and looked at her eye again.

"Did I do that?"

"No!" she said, quickly taking her hand off my face and putting it to her own.

"Do you promise?"

"Yes," she said. "I promise. I just walked into a door."

~ ~ ~

THE BIRD FEEDER was inches from my nose... I had probably been talking to it. I hoped I hadn't been eating birdseed.

I turned slowly, surveying the backyard. It was covered with snow. Tanner was sitting on the deck, watching me.

I walked across the yard. "Hi, Tanner."

"Hi, Dave," he smiled.

"Babysitting?" I asked, trudging up the steps.

"We prefer to call it 'Dave-sitting'."

"Fantastic. That sounds much better." I rolled my eyes at him. "Where's Laci?"

"She and Ashlyn went out to lunch."

"Well, good," I said, surprised. "I'm glad she's getting out and doing stuff."

"I made her go," Tanner explained.

"Oh," I said, nodding. "Thanks. Thanks for doing that."

"No problem," he said. "But she's gonna be sorry she missed you."

"Maybe I'll still be here when she gets back?"

"Maybe," he agreed. "It's hard to tell."

"Well, anyway, thanks."

"Sure. No problem."

I brushed snow off a chair and sat down.

"When did it snow?" I asked.

"Yesterday."

"First snowfall?"

"Second," he said. "We got a dusting last week."

"Is it . . . is it November?" I asked.

"The twenty-ninth," he nodded.

188

"I missed Thanksgiving?"

He nodded gently. I sat quietly for a moment, deciding not to find out who I had missed seeing.

"She really did a number on her eye, didn't she?" I asked after a minute.

"Yeah," he nodded.

"What exactly happened?" I asked casually. "She said something about slipping on the ice?"

"Yeah," he agreed, pointing toward the front of the house. "Fell right against the railing."

"Ouch," I said, shaking my head. "I sure am glad she didn't get hurt worse than she did."

"Yeah," Tanner said. "Me too."

~ ~ ~

LACI WAS STANDING right next to me. I was in the bathroom, brushing my teeth, and I looked at her in the mirror.

"You're doing good," she nodded encouragingly.

"Gee, thanks," I said wryly through a mouth full of toothpaste.

She looked at me questioningly but didn't say anything else. I finished brushing and then I rinsed and spit. I looked at her in the mirror again.

"It's me," I told her.

"I thought maybe it was," she smiled, stepping closer. I turned to face her and then I tucked a stray lock of hair behind her ear. I ran my finger gently over the skin under Laci's eye. Most of the swelling was gone, but her eye was still bloody and I could still see faint remains of the bruise under her skin.

"I did this," I told her.

She shook her head, pulling away from me slightly. "No."

"Yes, I did. I did this to you."

She swallowed hard and didn't say anything.

"I don't want you to keep things from me," I said. "I know you don't want to upset me and I know you're trying to protect me, but I wanna know the *truth*, okay?"

Tears welled up in her eyes and she nodded slightly.

"What happened?"

"You . . . you were upset," she began. "You didn't know who I was and you thought I was breaking into the house or something and you tried to call 9-1-1."

"And?"

"I tried to take the phone from you and you hit me."

190

I dropped my eyes to the ground for a moment and shook my head. Then I looked back up at her.

"I'm so sorry."

"It wasn't you." She smiled. "It was Anti-Dave."

"I don't like Anti-Dave," I told her.

"He's usually not so bad."

"How often do I get like that?"

"Not very often," she assured me. "I think it was one of the medicines you were on. We took you off it and nothing like that's happened since then."

"Okay," I nodded, stepping closer to her and stroking her hair, "but I meant what I said. I don't want you keeping things from me. From now on, if I ask you something, I want you to be honest with me . . . okay?"

"Okay."

"Promise?"

"I promise."

~ ~ ~

TANNER'S DOG, Winnie, was sitting next to me on the living room floor, letting me rub her ears.

"Hey, Winnie," I said, ruffling her fur. "How you doin' ol' girl?"

She licked my hand.

"Where's Laci?" I asked her. "Do you know where Laci is? Is your daddy babysitting? Where's your daddy?"

I rubbed her ear and she pressed her head against my hand appreciatively. I gave her a final pat and stood up.

It was dark outside. A game show was blaring on TV. I picked up the remote and turned it off.

"Where ya at, Tanner?"

"Down here," his voice came from the basement.

"Hi," I called.

"Hi," he called back. "I'll be right up."

"Take your time."

I heard the lid of the washing machine close and then the sound of his heavy feet, trudging up the stairs.

"Where's Laci?" I asked.

"Choir practice."

I nodded.

"Any chance I could get you to eat an apple?" he asked.

I looked at him questioningly.

"It would really make Laci happy if she gets home and finds out you ate an apple."

"Sure," I said. "I'll eat an apple."

"Great." He turned toward the kitchen.

"No!" I said sharply. "I can get it myself."

He turned back and looked at me.

"I'm not an invalid."

"I know," he said.

"Not yet, anyway," I muttered, walking past him.

I walked into the kitchen and grabbed an apple. I thought about cutting it up, but the whole process of finding a knife and figuring out how to use it seemed a little too much. I rubbed it off on my shirt and walked back into the living room.

Tanner was on the couch. He had taken over rubbing Winnie's head. I sat in my chair.

"I'm mad at you," I said, glaring at him.

"Why?" he asked. "Because I wanted to get you an apple?"

"No!" I snapped. "Because you *lied* to me."

"About what?"

"About Laci. About her eye."

"Oh," he said.

"I don't appreciate being lied to."

He looked at me.

"I mean it, Tanner. When I'm . . . when I'm *here*, I don't want to spend all my time wondering if everybody's lying to me."

"Laci didn't want me to tell you."

"Well, I don't care what Laci wanted," I said. "*I* want you to tell me the truth, so if I ask you something, I want you to tell me – okay?"

I expected him to nod, but he didn't.

"*Okay?*" I asked again.

"No," he said. "Actually, it's not okay."

I looked at him, surprised.

"What you're asking me to do," he said, "is to choose between the two of you. If you want one thing and Laci wants something else, then you're asking me to take your side."

"Look, I–"

"Is that really how you want it?" he interrupted. "Laci's gonna have a lot of hard decisions to make in the years ahead. Do you really want me giving her a hard time every time she has to decide something?"

I was quiet for a minute.

"No," I finally said. "Laci knows what I want, but if she needs to do something else . . . then I guess she should be able to do it."

"That's what I figured," Tanner said, nodding in a satisfied manner. "Now eat your apple. I wanna be able to show Laci an empty core when she gets home."

~ ~ ~

THE TV WAS on . . . another game show.

No wonder my mind was turning to drivel.

I looked around, wondering where Laci was.

I needed to go to the bathroom. I stood for a moment and got my bearings. I was okay by myself . . . I certainly hadn't forgotten how to go to the bathroom.

Just down that hall, first door on the right.

A few minutes later Laci found me in the bedroom.

"What are you doing?" she asked.

"Putting on big-people clothes."

"I don't think that's a good idea . . ."

"Laci, it's *me* – David! I don't need a *diaper.*"

"David, I–"

"Look, Laci," I said, raising my voice a little more than I meant to. "I understand that *Anti*-Dave might need a diaper, but right now I'm ME and I don't need a diaper."

"Okay," she said, raising her voice right back. "But how long are YOU going to be here?"

"I . . . I don't know," I admitted.

"No, you don't," she agreed. "And when Anti-Dave shows up again and he's not wearing a diaper then *I'm* the one who's gonna have a big mess to clean up."

We both stood there for a moment, staring at each other.

"I'm sorry," I finally said.

"No," she said. "I'm sorry. You should be able to wear what you want. I shouldn't have said that. I'm sorry."

I took a deep breath.

"I'll wear 'em."

"No, no . . ."

"Yes, I WANT to wear diapers. As a matter of fact, I can think of *nothing* more that I want to do right now than to wear diapers."

"They . . . they're actually called 'adult undergarments'."

"Well now, that makes it all better, doesn't it?"

She smiled at me.

"Can you get me a different brand?" I asked.

"Sure," she said, puzzled. "What do you want?"

"I don't know," I admitted, "but something very *sexy*. Anti-Dave and I still wanna look good for you."

TANNER AND LACI and I were all sitting together at the dining room table. We were having what appeared to be lunch.

"Hi," I said.

They both looked at me.

"Hi, *Tanner*," I clarified. "Hi, *Laci*."

"Hi," they both smiled.

"How you doing?" Tanner asked me.

"Fine," I said.

"Good," Tanner said. "I'll be back in a little bit."

"Where are you going?" I asked as he picked up his plate, which was still full of food.

"Winnie needs to go out," he said, heading to the kitchen.

"Tanner's here a lot," I observed after he'd gone onto the deck.

"Yes," she nodded.

"Isn't he missing work?"

"Tanner . . . he retired," she said hesitantly.

"He RETIRED?" I cried. "He's too young to retire!"

"He had thirty years in."

"But he was a *teacher*. He can't possibly have enough money to retire already. Is he going to do something else?"

"Yes."

"What?"

She looked at me and then took my hand.

"Come here," she said. "I want to show you something."

She led me to the guest bedroom. The closet door was open and it was full of clothes. A ball cap hung on the bedpost. Giant sneakers rested on the floor.

"Tanner's living here," I said slowly.

197

She nodded, squeezing my hand.

"And he's helping you," I said.

"Yes," she answered, pulling me into the hall. "Now come here."

She led me to our bedroom.

"This is ours," she said.

"I know."

"We sleep here . . . together," she explained. "I'm always here with *you*."

"I know," I said. "I didn't think anything else."

She looked relieved.

"I'm glad you have help," I assured her. "I'm glad it's Tanner."

She smiled and wrapped her arms around me.

"I'm glad you're back," she said.

~ ~ ~

TANNER WAS SITTING next to me – his chair pulled close to mine. His hand was resting gently on top of my arm and he was reading aloud from the Bible, which was propped up between us. He was reading from Genesis – the story of how Joseph's brothers had sold him into slavery and how eventually Pharaoh had put him in charge of the whole land of Egypt. Tanner was at the part where Joseph's brothers had come to Joseph for food during a famine – not realizing that he was their very own brother whom they had sold into slavery years before. Joseph had just set them up – hiding a silver cup in Benjamin's sack and insisting that Benjamin now become his slave. Judah was pleading with Joseph to allow Benjamin to return to their father Jacob with his other brothers – offering to stay as a slave in place of the boy.

> *"So now, if the boy is not with us when I go back to your servant*
> *my father and if my father, whose life is closely bound up with the boy's*
> *life, sees that the boy isn't there, he will die. Your servants will bring*
> *the gray head of our father down to the grave in sorrow. Your servant*
> *guaranteed the boy's safety to my father. I said, 'If I do not bring him*
> *back to you, I will bear the blame before you my father, all my life!'"*

Normally – when I suddenly found myself alone with Tanner – I would ask him how Laci was doing and – whenever I found myself alone with Laci – I would ask her how he was doing.

Tanner would always tell me that Laci was fine and she would always tell me that nothing had changed with Tanner.

(I also asked about Amber a lot and both of them always assured me that she was fine. I wasn't sure if I believed them, however,

199

because they also said the same thing about my dad, even though one day – when I'd been looking through the Bible where we kept birth announcements and stuff like that to see if Lily's baby had been born – I had found his obituary.)

But this time I didn't ask Tanner about Laci or my dad or Amber. Instead, I closed my eyes and I listened to him reading the Bible to me in his deep, resounding voice with the unfamiliar feel of his hand resting gently on my arm.

> *"No then, please let your servant remain here as my lord's slave in place of the boy, and let the boy return with his brothers. How can I go back to my father if the boy is not with me? No! Do not let me see the misery that would come upon my father."*

Tanner stopped reading. I opened my eyes.

"Why'd you stop?" I asked.

"I thought you were asleep," he said gently.

"No," I said, shaking my head.

He didn't say anything.

"Keep reading," I said. "This is my favorite part."

"Really? Why?" he asked with a little smile on his face as if he were humoring me.

"Because God is sovereign," I told him.

He looked at me questioningly, and I had the feeling that Anti-Dave didn't use words like "sovereign."

I closed my eyes and leaned my head back again.

"Keep reading."

It was silent for a moment and I knew that Tanner was trying to figure out just exactly whose arm his hand was on and exactly who he was reading the Bible to. After a moment he took his hand off my arm, but then he started reading again . . . finishing the story about how God works everything out for good.

~ ~ ~

I WAS SITTING in a pew at church – everybody else around me was standing. In my hand I held a length of cotton . . . the kind they pack into the top of pill bottles.

Tanner was standing next to me, holding a hymnal, and I looked up to find Laci singing in the choir.

I stood and put the cotton on the seat behind me.

Tanner looked at me.

"Hi, Tanner," I said quietly, trying to look on in his hymnbook with him.

"Hi, Dave," he said, moving it toward me. He pointed to where we were, but I had a hard time following along, so I finally gave up and just watched Laci singing.

After a moment she looked toward me and Tanner. She seemed surprised to see me standing there. I waved my hand at her and smiled.

She looked at me questioningly and raised her hand to sign to me.

Dave?

I nodded at her and smiled again.

She set her hymnal down behind her and hurried from the front of the church down to me.

"Hi," she whispered, hugging me.

"You didn't have to come down here," I said, whispering and hugging her back.

"It's almost over anyway."

"Go ahead back up there," I said. "I'll stick around."

"No thanks," she smiled. "I don't think I wanna take any chances."

After the service we walked outside. It was a beautiful day.

"It's spring, right?" I asked.

"Yep," Tanner said.

"Have I already had my birthday?" I asked.

"Yep."

"Did you make me a cake, Laci?" I asked.

"Of course I did!"

"Peanut butter, chocolate chip?"

She nodded and grinned.

"I'm sorry I wasn't there to enjoy it," I told her.

"Anti-Dave enjoyed it enough for both of you," she assured me as we reached the car. "Oh . . . wait! Did we get the cotton?"

"Got it," Tanner said, patting his jacket pocket.

"Why do we need cotton?" I asked.

"You *like* it," Tanner grinned. "It's very *soft*."

"It helps keep you busy during church," Laci explained.

"Yes," Tanner nodded as he unlocked the car. "It's something very *special* that we only let you have on Sundays."

"Please tell me that you're kidding."

"You're the one who wanted us to be honest with you," Tanner shrugged, holding the back door open for Laci. "I'll be glad to tell you that we all sit around discussing quantum physics if that'll make you feel better."

"Yeah, *right*," I muttered, climbing in after Laci. "As if *you* could discuss quantum physics."

Tanner closed the door and then got in up front.

I shook my head. *Cotton.*

"And where can your chauffer take you today?" Tanner asked, looking into the rearview mirror and tipping an imaginary cap at us.

"Are we still doing whatever makes me happy?" I asked Laci.

"Sure," she smiled.

"I wanna go to Cross Lake!" I said.

"Uhhh . . ."

202

"What?" I asked. "You don't want to go?

"No, sure," she said hesitantly. "I guess that'll be fine."

"So is that what we're doing?" Tanner asked uncertainly.

"Yeah," she said, still sounding concerned. "We can do that."

"What's the problem?" I asked.

"Nothing," she said as Tanner pulled out of the parking lot. "It's just that . . ."

"What?"

"It's an hour away," she explained.

"I know."

She looked at me knowingly.

"Oh," I said, finally understanding.

"But let's try it," she said. "If nothing else, it's a pretty day for a drive."

I was still with them an hour later when we arrived at the marina. We ordered burgers and onion rings and then Tanner untied his boat from the slip and we took off.

We cruised around the lake for a while, Tanner driving and Laci and me sitting up front, soaking in the sun.

After about twenty minutes we came to the island with the cabin on it that I had wanted to buy over twenty-five years earlier.

"It doesn't look like anyone's here this weekend," I said. "Can we pull in and look around for a while?"

"Sure," Laci agreed. Tanner pulled over to the dock, but didn't cut the motor.

"You guys go check it out," Tanner said. "I'm gonna go see if I can catch a few fish."

Laci and I got out.

"Call me if you need anything," Tanner said, acting as if he was talking to both of us, but clearly meaning Laci.

We nodded and waved and he pushed off and powered away.

"I guess he thinks I'm too stupid to notice that he doesn't have any fishing stuff?" I asked her.

She giggled and we held hands as we walked up the stone path.

"They used to have a woodbox," I explained to Laci as we walked around to the back. "That's how Tanner and I got in to see it that time."

"A woodbox?" she asked as we rounded the deck.

"Look!" I said when we got around to the back. "It's still here – you can still get in!"

"Don't get any bright ideas," Laci told me as I turned the latch.

"Come on!" I said. "I wanna look around!"

"No, David! Absolutely not!"

"Why not?" I asked, swinging the door open and peering in.

"Because it's called 'breaking and entering'!"

"That's what I told Tanner."

"And you still went in?"

"He made me!" I insisted. "Come on – let's check it out!"

"No!" she cried. "What if we get caught?"

"Oh, come on!" I urged. "Where's your sense of adventure?"

"I've had plenty of adventures lately, thank you very much."

"Look," I said. "My dementia is well documented. If anyone catches us you can say that I escaped and you've just found me and you're trying to take me home. I'll play dumb . . . really!"

She bit her lip and a mischievous look came into her eyes.

"Okay," she finally grinned, nodding.

"Wow!" I said, widening my eyes. "Laci Cline Holland actually breaking the law! You must *really* wanna make me happy!"

She smiled at me some more.

"I bet I could talk you into letting me have my way with you, too!"

"Don't get your hopes up," she said, but she was laughing. We crawled inside.

204

"It looks the same," I noted.

"It's beautiful," Laci said, looking around.

I slid open the door leading out onto the deck.

"The hot tub's still here!"

She shook her head at me. I walked over to it and opened the cover.

"It's ready to go!" I told her. "Let's get in!"

"There is *no way* we're getting in that hot tub!" she answered.

"Awww, come on, Laci!"

"What am I gonna tell the cops when they find us in the hot tub?"

"You were trying to save me from drowning and you took all your clothes off first so you wouldn't get them wet!"

"You really *are* out of your mind," she said, but she still had that mischievous look in her eyes and I realized that I actually had a decent shot of talking her into it. I found myself really wishing that I wasn't wearing an adult undergarment.

I put the lid back down and walked over to her, wrapping my arms around her waist.

"Remember how much you wanted to buy this place?" she asked, hugging me back.

"Yeah," I nodded. "That was right before we lost Amber."

"We got her back," she reminded me quietly.

"I know," I said.

We stood there, holding each other for a moment. I looked out, through the pine boughs, across the lake.

"I can't believe I thought living here would make me happy," I said, turning my eyes to Laci again. "Back then I really thought that this was what I wanted."

"And now what do you want?" Laci asked, looking up at me.

I looked back at her for a long, long moment before I replied.

"When we were little kids," I finally said, "God told you to love me. And for all these years, no matter *what*, you've always loved me.

Even when I'm gone and Anti-Dave shows up or something, you're still always waiting for me to come back and you always love me."

"I love Anti-Dave too," she smiled.

"So what more could I ever want?"

~ ~ ~

I WOKE UP in our bedroom, the light on the dresser shining dimly. I was all alone in bed.

"Laci?" I called out.

"David!" I heard her say. I turned toward her voice. She was to my right, sitting up in a twin bed that was next to our queen.

"Why are you over there?" I asked her as she left her bed and crawled under the covers with me.

"Anti-Dave sleeps better alone," she explained, wrapping her arms around me and pressing her head against my shoulder.

"Let me guess," I said. "He sleeps better with the lights on too?"

She lifted her head and nodded, smiling slightly at me.

The hall light came on and Tanner appeared in our doorway.

"Everything okay?" he asked.

"Yeah," Laci answered. "We're fine."

"Hi, Tanner," I said.

He smiled. "Hi, Dave."

Then he closed the door behind him before he headed back down the hall.

~ ~ ~

A GAME SHOW was playing on the television.

"What force must be overcome when a stationary object is put into motion?"

"Static friction," I answered. I glanced over and found Tanner staring at me with his mouth slightly open.

"Hi, Tanner!"

"Apparently nerdy, geeky Dave is back?" he asked.

"Apparently," I smiled.

"I'm gonna call Laci and let her know," he said, reaching for his phone.

"Where is she?"

"She's over at Jessica's," he explained. "Chris had a hip replacement yesterday."

"Oh."

"Hey, Laci," he said. "I've got somebody here who wants to talk to you!"

He handed me the phone.

"Hi, Laci."

"Oh, David! Oh, I'm so sorry I'm not there."

"That's okay," I said. "No problem."

"I'm gonna come home right now, okay? I'll be there in about fifteen minutes."

"Take your time," I said. "No hurry."

I closed the phone and handed it to Tanner.

"She's gonna be sorry she wasn't here," he said, shaking his head.

"I'll probably still be here when she gets home, won't I?" I asked.

"I don't know," Tanner said dubiously.

"I was back for like eight hours the other day."

He looked at me skeptically.

"When we went to the lake?" I reminded him.

He thought about it for a moment and then said, gently, "That was eight months ago."

"It was?"

He nodded.

"Are you sure?" I asked.

"I'm sure."

"I can't believe that," I said quietly. "It feels like it was last week."

We sat there for a moment.

"I haven't been back much since then, have I?" I finally asked, trying to remember.

"You've been back some," he assured me.

"But I don't stay long?"

"Not usually," he admitted, "or you don't remember it the next time."

I sighed.

"Wanna see something?" Tanner asked.

"Sure."

He opened his phone and showed me a picture.

"Look," he said, handing it to me and leaning over the back of my chair. "That's Dorito."

"I know," I said defensively. Dorito was standing with a bunch of people I didn't recognize and holding a giant pair of scissors. "What's he doing?"

"See this ribbon?" Tanner asked, pointing.

"Yeah."

"This was the ribbon-cutting ceremony for the new wing at the orphanage."

"*Really?*"

"Yeah!"

"That's great," I smiled.

"Here, look," he went on, scrolling through the pictures on the phone that was in my hand. He came to a close-up of a sign. It said:

In honor of David and Laci Holland.

"They dedicated it to *us?*" I asked.

"Yeah," Tanner said.

"They shouldn't have done that," I said, shaking my head.

"That's *exactly* what Laci said," he laughed.

"Did Laci go?"

"No," he said. "They invited both of you to come and everything, but we thought it was going to be too hard on you to go."

"Aw, Tanner," I said, looking back over my shoulder at him. "You should have made her go at least."

"I tried," Tanner insisted, walking back to his chair. "She wouldn't leave you."

"I hate that," I said as Tanner sat back down. "She should have been there for that."

"No," he said, shaking his head. "It was better that she didn't go. That was actually the weekend we went to the lake."

"Really?" I asked.

"Yeah, really," he said, a big smile crossing his face. "That was the greatest day for Laci. She wouldn't have missed that for the world!"

I looked at him for a long moment.

"You still love her," I said to him.

He looked back at me, surprised.

"You've always loved her," I went on.

Finally Tanner spoke, carefully choosing his words.

"I . . . I've always wanted what's best for Laci."

"You love her."

"I want what's *best* for her," he said again.

"You're not denying that you love her," I told him matter-of-factly.

He looked at me for another long moment.

"*You're* what's best for her," he finally told me. "You've always been what's best for her."

~ ~ ~

IT WAS A madhouse and clearly Christmas. I looked around, trying to see if all the kids had made it. The living room was full of granddaughters.

Dorito was walking past me toward the kitchen wearing a red and white Santa hat.

"Merry Christmas, Dorito," I said, stepping toward him.

He stopped to look at me and then a huge smile spread across his face.

"Merry Christmas, Dad!" he said, hugging me tight. "How're you doing?"

"I think I'm pretty good," I answered. "Can I wear your hat?"

~ ~ ~

I WAS CONFUSED. It took me a while to figure out that I was lying in a hospital bed, all alone.

"Laci?" I called out, as loudly as I could.

"David?"

I hadn't been alone after all . . . she was sleeping in a chair next to my hospital bed.

"It's me," I told her. "I'm back."

"I know," she smiled.

"Why am I here?" I asked.

"You . . . you had to have some surgery," she said hesitantly.

"For what?"

"Cancer," she said, fighting back the tears.

"What kind?"

"Colon cancer."

"I had *surgery?*"

She nodded.

I had a sinking feeling that in addition to an adult undergarment I was now also wearing a colostomy bag. I started to ask, but then decided that I didn't really want to know.

"Did they get it all?" I asked.

"No," she said, shaking her head, "but they're going to do some chemo and the doctors say–"

"Chemo? *What?* No! No chemo!"

"David . . ."

"I do *not* want chemotherapy . . . do you understand?"

"David, I–"

"Why did you even let them do surgery?" I cried. "I can't believe Tanner went along with this!"

"We talked to Mike about it—"

"Is this really what you want, Laci?" I interrupted. "You want me to go through chemo? For what? So you can spend the next five years having me back for fifteen minutes every few months?"

She started sobbing.

"We just need to let it go."

"I can't." She cried harder and buried her head against me (which hurt – I guess because I'd just had surgery).

"Laci," I whispered, trying to stroke her hair with my hand. An IV tube that was sticking out of the back of my hand caught on the bed rail. I switched hands.

"Laci," I said again, gently lifting her head.

"What?" she managed to ask.

"I wanna talk to Mike. Can you get Mike on the phone for me?"

She nodded.

"Hurry," I told her.

She pushed some buttons and held the phone out toward me with a shaking hand.

"Hi, Mike," I said. "It's David."

"Hi, Dave. How are you?"

"It's really me . . . do you understand?"

"Yeah. I understand."

"Okay . . . well, I need you to do me a favor."

"What's that?"

"I don't want any more treatments . . . I don't want *anything* done to prolong this. Do you understand what I'm saying?"

"I understand what you're saying, but you really need to talk to Laci about it. She's the one that's gotta decide all this stuff."

"I *have* talked to her, but she's gonna need some help doing this. That's all I'm saying. Can you promise me that you'll help her?"

"Yeah," he said quietly. "I promise."

"Thanks, Mike. You're a good friend. You've always been a good friend."

214

He didn't say anything and Laci choked down another sob.

"Are you there?"

"Yeah," he managed. "I'm here."

"It'll be alright. I'll see you again, okay?"

"Okay."

"Thanks."

I hung up and looked at Laci. Her eyes were still full of tears.

"You just listen to Mike. You do what Mike says, okay?"

She nodded and wiped her eyes. I tilted my head at her.

"Your hair . . ." I said after a moment.

"What about it?"

"How long has it been since I was diagnosed?"

"With cancer?"

"No . . ."

"Oh," she said. She thought about it for a moment. "I guess about five years."

"Really?"

She nodded.

"It doesn't seem like that long," I smiled at her. Then I said, "It probably seems like a lot longer to you, doesn't it?"

"No," she said, shaking her head, tears welling up again.

"So, how come your hair hasn't changed?" I asked. (It was at stage two – my favorite stage.)

"What do you mean?"

"I mean . . . it looks the same as when we left Mexico. I don't remember it changing this whole time. Haven't you been sending it to Locks of Love?"

"No," she said, shaking her head. "When you got diagnosed I decided to keep it the same. I thought that maybe it would help to keep you from getting so confused."

I laughed out loud and I think I pulled a stitch or something because it really hurt.

"It didn't help much!" I said. She smiled back at me. "Actually, now that I think about it, that's probably what's wrong with me in the first place."

"What do you mean?"

"I think that's why you started cutting off all your hair way back in preschool," I said. "Just so you could mess with my head."

~ ~ ~

IT WAS DARK . . . or maybe my eyes were closed. Laci was holding my hand and talking to me. Something about Gabby.

I wanted to let her know that I was back so I tried to say her name, but my mouth was so dry.

Laci kept talking. Now she was saying something about my mom and my dad . . . something about Greg and Mr. White. It was hard to concentrate on what she was saying because I was trying so hard to talk.

"Laci . . ." I finally managed. My voice sounded so hoarse.

"David!" she cried and I felt her hand on my face. She kissed me. "I love you so much . . ."

"I love you, too."

"But I want you to know that it's okay," she said, squeezing my hand. "You don't have to stay. You can go to Jesus, David. It's okay. Go see Gabby and your mom and your dad and Mr. White–"

"You'll be okay," I stated.

"Yes," she said. She was crying. "I'll be okay . . . I promise. I'll be okay."

I believed her.

"Go see Greg," she said. "Go see Jesus . . ."

"I see him," I told her.

"*Who?*" she cried.

I wondered why she sounded so surprised.

"You see who?" she asked again. "*Jesus? Greg?*"

But my voice wouldn't work anymore, so I just nodded at her. And I think I smiled.

And then I went.

The End

~ ~ ~

Will Tanner ever commit his heart to the Lord? Does Jordan have Huntington's disease? What happens to Laci after David dies? Did they really get Amber back, and if so, how did that happen and what in the world is going on with her?

Although *Gone* is the final book to be told by David, it is not the last book in the *Chop, Chop* series. All of these questions and more will be answered in the last two books of the series: a few in Book 7 (*Not Quickly Broken*) and most in Book 8 (*Alone*). I sincerely hope that you will join Jordan and Tanner, respectively, for these last two novels – I look forward to sharing them with you!

In Christ's love,
L.N. Cronk

CPSIA information can be obtained
at www.ICGtesting.com
Printed in the USA
LVHW111034310522
720044LV00024B/418